Lock Down Publications and Ca$h
Presents

Crime Boss 4
POINT OF NO RETURN

Written By
Playa Ray

First Edition 2024

Printed in the United States of America

Lock Down Publications
P.O. Box 944
Stockbridge, GA 30281
www.lockdownpublications.com

Like our page on Facebook: Lock Down Publications
www.facebook.com/lockdownpublications.ldp

Stay Connected with Us!

Text **LOCKDOWN** to 22828 to stay up-to-date with new releases, sneak peaks, contests and more…

Like our page on Facebook:
Lock Down Publications

Join Lock Down Publications/The New Era Reading Group

Visit our website:
www.lockdownpublications.com

Follow us on Instagram:
Lock Down Publications

Email Us: We want to hear from you!

Acknowledgement

This book is dedicated to my best friend, Loquez Bell. The streets will never be the dame without you, my brother. I told you my plan, and you can trust that I'm gonna stick to it, no matter what. Just keep watching me from your heavenly throne. Much love!!

"Loyalty is not just a word—it's a lifestyle. Live by it!!
-Jane Pennella
Hillsboro, Oregon

Chapter 1

Monday

"And how did Manning respond to that?" Ebony asked Samantha, who was seated across the table from her in the cafeteria.

Samantha took a sip of her lemonade to wash her food down, before answering, "Girl, you know how Manning is. She chewed my ass out in front of the whole courtroom."

"I take it that you were embarrassed?"

There was a simper on Ebony's face.

"Only because Hendrix was there."

Ebony smirk evaporated. "Why was Hendrix there?"

"He was on miscellaneous duty," explained Samantha, now grinning like a teenaged school girl. "At his leisure, he stopped in to see how I was doing."

"Is that what he told you?" Ebony posed, hating the question the second it rolled off her tongue. For sure she knew that this was her chance to avert Samantha's feelings away from Albert Spires, but it seemed like she was more concerned with preventing her friend from falling for the new assistant district attorney.

"Yes, that's what he told me," Samantha responded, with much attitude. "And, what's with the acrimony you have toward him? You haven't said one nice thing about Hendrix since he's been here."

"He has nice hair," Ebony offered, to lighten the mood, then forked a portion of pasta salad into her mouth.

5

"Very funny."

"I'm serious," she avowed, after taking a sip of her iced tea. "In fact, he has an award-winning personality, and he's handsome. You may think I'm blowing smoke, but I actually believe you two would make a nice pair."

Samantha made a face. "He's married."

Ebony matched her expression. "And you never been with a married man before?"

Samantha furrowed her eyebrows but said nothing.

"Come on, Sam," Ebony pressed. "Don't act like you haven't considered asking him out."

"Of course, I have," the redhead replied, conspiringly. "But, I have also considered that he may not be the type to step out on his wife."

"Girl, please!" Ebony let out. "From the moment that man laid eyes on you, he's been following you around like a love-sick puppy. I'm surprised he hasn't popped the question himself."

"And what if he finally decided to do so?" Samantha posed, now regarding her friend askance. "What am I to expect out of you?"

"My full support."

Samantha maintained her visage.

"Look, Sam," Ebony resumed. "As long as you don't let anyone destroy what we have, we'll always have that. Of course, I get jealous at times, but it only shows that I'm human. And don't act like you don't got your own jealous spells."

The redhead now had a devilish grin on her face. "I plea the Fifth," she asserted, raising her right hand as if being sworn in.

"Yeah, you better!" Ebony responded, laughing, gendering at her watch. "I have to retrieve some files from my office before returning to the courtroom. Should I wait for you after work?"

"If you're released early," Samantha told her, "go on home. Just call me before you go to bed."

Ebony made the journey to her office, but not to retrieve any files as she'd purported to Samantha. It was a little after onePM, and her early morning high had evaporated a couple of hours ago. Therefore, she needed to refuel her system with the powered drug that she'd become dependent upon, to get her through each day.

Making sure to lock the door upon entering the office, Ebony flopped down into her leather chair, unlocked the bottom drawer of her desk, and fetched the vial containing crush. At this time, it seemed like her need for the drug had augmented, whereas her mouth had become watery as she sprinkled some on top of some document that was already on her desk. She used her identification card to divide it into two lines but, before she could treat herself, the desk phone began to ring.

For a moment, Ebony just stared at the device as if seeing it for the first time. Then, thinking it was Samantha, she quickly snatched the receiver from its cradle.

"Linton County District Attorney's Office!" she promulgated with formality; in case it was someone other than her friend. "Assistant District Attorney Ebony Davis speaking."

"Thank God I caught you!" exclaimed a familiar feminine voice. "I thought I'd have to leave you a message which is something I'm not a fan of, I tell you. So, how are you Ms. Davis?"

"I'm fine," Ebony answered, trying to place the voice with its thick southern drawl. "And with whom am I speaking to?"

"Oh! Pardon my manners," the caller said, apologetically. "This is Attorney Lisa Wortham, and I was calling to give you an update on the case, and to go over some things with you."

"Okay." Ebony checked her watch, seeing that she had approximately twenty-three more minutes left before having to return to the courtroom.

She then placed her I.D. card beside the readied drug before leaning back in her chair with the receiver pressed to the side of her face.

"At this point," the attorney began, "a summon has been issued to Pharmacy of America Laboratories in Wisconsin. My colleagues and I are currently compiling a list of physicians who've had any kind of knowledge of the deadly drug. However, we've come across a doctor by the name of Willie McAdams. Are you familiar with him?"

"I am," she answered, now thinking about the conversation she had with him this past Sunday.

"So, you are aware if him being your grandmother's medical consultant?"

"Well," Lisa Wortham continued, "we were able to access Doctor McAdams' financial records, which did not align with his ledger, with respect to the medical treatment provided to the late Mrs. Regina Davis. Also, Mr. McAdams has several tort claims brought against him in other states for malpractice, which would make him the perfect defendant in this case. But, as I said, his financial records are not in accordance with his ledger, when it comes to validating treatment for Mrs. Davis."

"Explain!" Ebony prompted, not liking what she was hearing so far.

She wet the tip of her index finger, in which she used to taste the powered drug that was still awaiting her, before leaning back in her chair, to continue listening to the attorney.

"According to Mr. McAdams' ledger," she went on, "he was assigned to Mrs. Regina Davis in the year of two thousand and one, succeeding Dr. Marla Hansley. This same record shows that he received his monthly fees and payments for treatment, via a joint account belonging to a Mr. Terrence and Regina Davis up until August of two thousand and five. Now regarding this account, one would automatically assume that the physician and patient had severed their ties at that time. However, a closer inspection would show that the physician was still rendering treatment to the patient, although there's no sign of any form of payment transaction between the two."

"Are you saying that he was giving her free treatment?" Ebony posed, pressing speaker phone before placing the receiver into its cradle.

She then scooped some of the drug into the fingernail of her pinky and inhaled it through her left nostril.

"Well," the attorney's voice sounded through the phone's speaker, as Ebony was treating her other nostril, "it appears that way up until two thousand and twenty-three, which provides that Mr. McAdams received his regular monthly payment from the same joint account belonging to Mr. and Mrs. Davis. In the following month, he received the same payment and placed an order to Pharmacy of America Laboratories in Wisconsin for their new product, Xycobin."

She paused to clear her throat. "Excuse me! Now, this is where it gets more cabalistic. Although the record shows that McAdams ordered the drug, it doesn't reveal for whom he ordered it for, being that it was purchased from his very own account."

So, how were you able to determine that my grandmother had been taking the drug?" Ebony want to know. She was absently thrumming a finger on her desk.

"It's in her medical records," Wortham let on. "It doesn't say who the prescriber was—only that the medicine was ordered from the Pharmacy of America Laboratories. Every case we're pursuing were initially dug up by our investigator."

"So, these people basically used my grandmother as an experimental lab rat."

"I wouldn't use that exact term," the attorney tried to reason. "But we do believe that the drug had not undergone a proper experimental inspection before being distributed to its intended recipients."

"From what you've told me so far," Ebony spoke at a length, "it seems as if you all don't have enough on Dr. McAdams to solidify him as a defendant in the case. As id he'll come out of this ordeal unmolested."

"It's possible," the attorney admitted with a sigh. "However, although it seems as if he was trying to conceal his involvement, we're not letting up on him. He's just as guilty as the manufacturer, and we're determined to prove it."

"I sure hope so."

Chapter 2

Anthony was still livid about Ebony sending one of her goons to interfere with his personal affairs on Saturday. Especially after he had everything perfectly planned out. This had him holed up in his motel room, all day, Sunday, watching the news channel to see if he'd suddenly become a fugitive of the law. Though he watched the recap of his incident over twenty times, nothing seemed to change. There was still only one witness claiming to have seen a dark-colored car fleeing the scene after hearing shots fired from what sounded like a sub-machine gun.

The identity of the perpetrator was still unknown, but the victim was identified as twenty-six-year-old Zoey Daniels of College Park, Georgia, which was strange to Anthony, being that he didn't remember any of Ebony's 'workers' being from anywhere near the Atlanta area. Were there more close by?

After surprisingly getting a good night's rest, Anthony was astir before eightAM With the television still on the news channel, he turned the volume all the way up so he could hear it while showering. As far as he could tell, he was still unidentifiable.

Today's the day that Anthony was scheduled to take the rental car back to its owners. It's also the day that he planned on taking a drive back to Macon, Georgia. After washing and getting dressed, he donned his coat and carried all of his belongings from the room to his Lincoln Innovator. He'd even placed the P.98, which he'd cleaned and swaddled in one of the motel's bedspreads, into the trunk to discard at his earlies convenience. Once he was sure that he had everything, Anthony climbed into the rental, and drove out of the parking lot.

Being that the rental dealership was just right up the street, it had taken Anthony less than ten minutes to reach it. After signing the car back in, he exited the establishment, hoping that his ballcap and sunglasses would avail him in being unnoticeable to anyone who may easily recognize him from anywhere as he walked back towards the motel, in the fifty-something degree weather.

"Good morning, sir!" the motel's receptionist greeted, when he entered the office, moments later. "Is everything okay with your room?"

"Everything's fine," Anthony replied, handing him the plastic key. "Thanks for having me!"

"Any time sir."

Finally secure of his own car, Anthony made sure to order himself some breakfast from the drive-thru of a nearby restaurant before heading for the expressway. But, as he neared the expressway, he was overwhelmed with the notion that he'd left something. Not at the motel, but at his mother's home. Though he was not certain of what it may be. However, given that this notion was strong, he changed course and made for Johnson Street.

Parking at the curb, Anthony dismounted and rushed towards the house where he used his own keys to gain entrance. After disarming the alarm, he headed for his old bedroom. The door was standing wide open. Anthony entered and stood around not knowing exactly what he was looking for, though he immediately noticed that the room had been changed back to how it was on the night he arrived, except there was a different bedspread, and the toys were neatly put aside.

Still unaware of what he was looking for, Anthony exited the room making for his mother's bedroom where the door was slightly ajar. Pushing it open, he took two steps inside and stopped with his hand still on the doorknob. The room was tidy as always with the faint scent of his mother's perfume lingering in the air.

At that moment, Anthony thought about the gun in his trunk that he needed to get rid of and began backing out of the room. But as he was pulling the door shut, a manila folder atop the dresser caught his attention causing him to stop in his tracks. Maybe, it was because the folder was incongruous amongst the panoply of cosmetic items.

Inquisitive, Anthony moved towards the dresser, where he retrieved the folder, and open it. There was one piece of paper inside, whereas the words: LINKTON COUNTY HEALTH CLINIC seemed to jump out at him. Then there was 'Origin DNA Testing', followed by his, and the name of Tyrone Terrence Davis, with DECEASED beside the latter. Reluctantly, he shifted his gazed down to the results that read: 0.00%.

Anthony must've reread the document a dozen times. In fact, he was so engrossed in the sole piece of paper, he didn't remember taking a seat on the edge of his mother's bed. Finally tired of torturing himself with the contents of the paper, he closed the folder and sat it down beside himself while his mind ran rampant. There were a million and one questions, with just as many evil thoughts clouding his mental at the moment. It seemed like everything was starting to take a wrong turn in his life.

Anthony didn't know that he'd been sitting in the same spot for hours, until his mother appeared in the doorway, clad in her uniform and her pocketbook hanging off her shoulder. He was furious, so he could pretty much imagine the look that he was regarding her with. Carol shifted her gaze to the folder that was obviously not in the same place she'd left it. Drawing a breath, she sagely crossed the room and took a seat on the bed, not bothering to remove her coat or pocketbook. Anthony diverted his attention unable to look at the woman whom he felt has betrayed him.

"I don't know what to tell you," Carol spoke in almost a whisper.

"How about the truth?" He offered, turning on her with the same menacing look. "For all of these years, you've fed me this B.S. about Tyrone being my father, and now I come to find out he's not."

"I know who I was with when you were conceived, Anthony," she replied through clenched teeth.

Anthony folded the top flap of the folder open on the bed. "Apparently not!" he contended. "I don't think these results are false."

Now visibly angry herself, Carol just stared at her son as tears streamed down her face.

"And how long have you had these results?" he pushed.

She wiped at the tears with the back of her hand before answering. "Ebony brought it to me on the day she visited. The same day she came down to the jail to see you."

Astounded, Anthony slowly rose from the bed, and was now looking down at his mother. "And you didn't tell me about this shit? What else are you keeping from me?"

Anthony almost revealed his knowledge of his mother still being in contact with Janelle but caught himself. Instead, he marched out of the room, slamming the front door behind him upon exiting the house.

Back in the car, he drove for the expressway, wondering how things between him and his mother would be from then on. For this was the only person he ever really trusted and believed in. How could she betray him? And why would Ebony withhold the results from him by claiming they were still unclear? What did she expect to gain by deceiving him?

Chapter 3

The Run-fit gym had a decent size crowd. After completing her laps around the indoor track, Ebony took twenty minutes to cool down before receiving her pocketbook and coat from the locker they'd provided her as a member of their establishment. Though it was dark out, the parking lot was well-lit with lamps. She started her car by remote, but climbed into the front passenger seat of Rick's car that was parked two cars from hers.

Rick had his seat reclined and didn't bother to look in her direction as he appeared to be staring into outer space through the windshield. He wasn't the type to display his true feelings, but Ebony assumed he was upset about having to drive out to meet her on such a short notice.

"I'm listening," Rick said, the moment she slammed the passenger's door, still looking straight ahead.

"I received a call from that lawyer put in Texas," Ebony apprised.

When he didn't reply, she went on to expound what the attorney explained to her.

"So," Rick said. Once she was done, "you don't think that this doctor will get what he deserves for his involvement?"

"Not through the court system," she answered, gazing out the side window. "That's why we'll be paying him a visit tomorrow night."

"You can't be serious."

Ebony turned to see that he was now looking at her, his brown eyes half-hooded by his narrow eyebrows. "You think I'm not?" she posed.

"I just hope you're not."

"Are you breaching our contract, Rick?"

"No," he answered. "I'm thinking rationally."

"Oh?"

"Trust me," Rick told her. "I am not against you retaliating against dude. But his death would raise a lot of suspicion. Especially with that law firm, right after having a conversation about him."

Ebony knew that he was right but defied to admit it. Instead, she averted her gaze back out the side window.

"I can see that you're out for blood right now," he acknowledged. "If it'll make you feel better, we can go after Anthony, tonight. Call your tracker and get his location. With or without Bull, we can drive to Atlanta and get this over with."

Ebony didn't linger for one second. She quickly fished the pre-paid cellular from her pocketbook sitting in her lap, pulled Zoe's number up on her contacts lists and pressed call. Reggae music played in her ear. Succinctly before his voicemail came on. Not interested in leaving a message, she tried again, only to get the same results.

"He's not answering," she intoned, replacing the phone.

"I have to go home and get ready," Rick told her. "Try again when you get home. Once you get the coordinates, let me know, and I'll be on my way. Are we excluding Bull?"

"Hell no!" responded Ebony. "He's equally entitled to honor this contract just as you are. And if he has a problem with that, he can be next."

On that note Ebony dismounted, and stormed off towards her car that was still running. The console was warm when she climbed inside, tossing her pocketbook onto the front passenger seat. Rick was pulling off while Ebony was contemplating dialing Zoe's number, again. Finally deciding that she would wait until she got home, Ebony drove on, unaware that she was being watched through the windshield of the green, older model Cadillac, though the driver chose not to follow her this time.

Making it home, Ebony headed straight for her bedroom, where she doffed her gym clothes. Now down to her underwear, she retrieved the pre-paid phone, and called Zoe only to acquire his voicemail again. Tossing the device onto the bed, she headed for the main bathroom to take her shower, hoping that if Zoe was busy at the moment he would be 'unbusy' by the time she was done.

Almost thirty minutes later, with nothing but a towel wrapped around her body, and one around her head, Ebony re-entered her bedroom, deciding that she would try Zoe's number again before getting dressed. But, when she grabbed the phone off the bed, she saw that there was a text message from Rick, which came in seven minutes ago. She opened it: *CALL ME ASAP!*

Ebony did just that.

"Are you watching the World News?" Rick asked upon answering the phone.

"No," she replied, moving towards the dresser for her cosmetic items. "I just got out of the shower. What's on the World News?"

"Look for yourself."

Ebony frowned at his sarcasm as she looked around for the remote control to the television that she couldn't remember the last time watching. Relinquishing the unsuccessful attempt, she walked over to the 47-inch TV mounted on the wall and presses the power button. After *NU-VISION* sat in the center of the screen for what seemed like an eternity. She was able to navigate it to the appropriate channel before taking a few steps back and allowing her eyes to adjust to the brightness of it.

Suddenly, a wave of nausea came over her as she stared at ta picture of Zoe, who seemed to be staring back at her.

Twenty-six-year-old Zoey Daniels, according to the disembodied male anchorman, was murdered in Marrietta, Georgia while sitting in his car that was parked on English Avenue. A witness, after hearing multiple gunshots, was only able to see a dark-colored car fleeing the scene. There were no leads on any suspects.

"Are you there?" Rick's voice came through the earpiece.

"Yeah," Ebony answered. "Isn't English Avenue…?"

"The next street from it," he answered her unasked question.

"You think Anthony made him?" She knew that it was an asinine question but pit it out there to see what kind of feedback she'd get from Rick.

"Unless your man chose to take his own life, one street over from the street that Anthony had been stalking," Rick responded.

Moving away from the television, Ebony sat on the edge of the bed.

"Give me your take on this."

"I can assure you that he was already expecting for you to send somebody after him," Rick told her. "That's why he was able to spot your man. At that moment, he knew that it was either kill, or be killed, and he chose to come out on top. Now, in his mind, it's war between you two. So, he'll either find another location to lay low in or come after you."

"But I know where his mother lives," Ebony pointed out. "And he's aware of this."

"Which is why I believe he's gonna come after you."

Chapter 4

Last night, after getting off the phone with Rick, who offered to have some men to watch her house—to which she declined—Ebony got dressed and fixed herself something to eat. Rick's caveat of Anthony coming after her didn't bother her one bit, though she made sure that every door and window were secure, and that her gun was ready to fire at will.

No, she wasn't worried, but she was definitely livid. How could Zoe allow himself to be spotted by Anthony? Even worse, how could he even allow Anthony to get the drop on him like that? His mission was to monitor and report Anthony's movements, but Ebony could only blame herself for not moving in on the traitor when she had the chance, even if it meant causing harm to his mother and son.

After picking over her dinner, ebony knew she couldn't fully relax until after fueling her system with crush, but the drug alone wouldn't suffice, which compelled her to break seal on the bottle of Maker's 46 that Jason had purchased prior to his demise. Ebony had gotten so caught up in drinking, getting high, and toiling over her problems, she didn't remember falling asleep. She remembered being awakened by her galling alarm clock and forcing herself out of bed only to arrive thirty minutes late for work. It was just surprising that Barbara Hutchins didn't chew her out for her tardiness.

"Is the State in opposition of the request made by the defense?" Judge Jackson asked, bringing Ebony back to the present day.

"Of course," she responded, sniffing back a drainage, and wiping her nose with the back of her hand. She remained seated at her table. "Probation would be utterly out of the question for Mr. Dinkins, who was a recipient of probation back in two thousand and nineteen, which was set to conclude some time in two thousand and twenty-two. However, Mr. Dinkins violated that compact in two thousand and twenty-one by committing the act of burglary, which was the same offense that spawned the in-home supervision."

"Do you have documentation to support your argument?"

"Would I be saying this if I didn't?" Ebony shot back.

The judge narrowed her eyes at her. "You're skating on a fairly thin ice, Ms. Davis. It would behoove you to maintain professional conduct from this moment on. Now, again, do you have documentation to support your argument?"

"Yes, I do," Ebony rejoined, refusing to add 'Your Honor'.

He directed his attention to the defense table, where a dark hair attorney sat with her client, who was clad in an orange jail issued jumpsuit.

"Can the defense confute argument made by the State in regards to the defendant's prior placement and revocation of probation?"

"No, Your Honor," the attorney answered, remaining in her seat. "In fact, the defense does not deny prosecutor's findings. However, being that my client had been punished for the violation, we are asking if the court would disregard this and grant Mr. Dinkins probation for this current charge, which is non-violent, and has no relation to the aforementioned incident."

"Your Honor," Ebony was loath to say, "To grant the defense such request would tread upon the guidelines created by lawmakers with respect to habitual violators being allowed to serve a second term on probation."

"And what statue are you basing your assertion off of?" the judge inquired.

"One that I am unable to quote at this moment." Ebony knew it was a mistake but refused to succumb to it. "However, such statute does exist."

"Well," Judge Jackson started, an amused smirk on his face, "If the State can't produce anything to support this, then the argument is without merit."

"The State shouldn't have to put forth anything supportive of this claim," Ebony retorted, regarding him with her own amused expression, "because the court should know better that to…"

"I beg your pardon!" he growled, cutting her off, now looking as if he was ready to pounce on her.

"At this time," she spouted, "the State has no additional facts to support its argument."

The older man seem to stare into her soul for an eon before saying, "Very well. Mr. Dinkins will receive fifteen years for burglary, to be served on probation. State if you would go ahead and process the disposition we could adjourn for the day." He looked to Deputy Taylor, who was standing to the right of him. "This is the last one right?"

Taylor nodded that it was.

While Ebony was filling out the final disposition form, she overheard Taylor and Jackson discussing a golf game with Briggs this coming Saturday. Once she was done, the responsible parties signed it, the Deputy Taylor escorted the defendant back to the holding cell, where the other inmates were waiting to be transferred back to the county jail. Judge Jackson shot Ebony another menacing look before retiring to his chambers, but she brushed it off and continued gathering her things into her briefcase.

"You're a real live one," commented Larry Hendrix, who was now standing beside the State's table. He'd been seated at the rear of the courtroom for over an hour. "If I were to do a poll, I think it would prove that female prosecutors are more aggressive than male prosecutors."

Despite how she was feeling, Ebony did manage to smile at the statement. Snapping her briefcase shut, she stood and locked eyes with the prosecutor. "Are you Mrs. Hutchin's emissary today?" she questioned with raised eyebrows. "Did she send you in here to spy on me?"

"If she did send me in here to spy on you," he responded, "I wouldn't be too much of any use because she'll end up hearing about what happened in this courtroom today before I could get back to her. Hell, I bet the judge is halfway to ger office right now."

"Snitching on me huh?" Ebony replied, prompting laughter from Hendrix just as Taylor re-entered the room via the side door.

"Do you have to stop by your office before leaving?" Hendrix asked her.

"I sure do."

"Then I guess we'll travel together."

"Sounds good to me!" she said loud enough to be heard by Taylor, displaying a broad, plausible smile as she strutted with a purpose towards the entrance followed by Hendrix.

Ebony didn't know what kind of game Taylor was playing but if he called himself playing hardball with her, then she was definitely going to make him regret making that decision.

"So, what did the Wicked Witch of the West have you doing all day?" Ebony asked Hendrix as they walked to the corridor to the elevators.

"Scrubbing toilets and cleaning gutters," he answered, winning an incredulous look from her. "Okay. Maybe not. After a few plea and arraignment hearings in Judge Stewart's courtroom, I spent some time with Officer Towns in the evidence room."

"And what could you have possibly been doing in the evidence room?" Ebony asked, ringing for the elevator that appeared immediately.

"It was the boss' idea," he answered, entering the empty shaft behind Ebony. "I guess she didn't feel as if I'd seen enough of it on my first visit. However, this visit was quite enlightening. I remember seeing the footage of what happened to your father on the news, but to see it again after nineteen years…I don't know. I guess it was like an eye opener to what could possibly happen to anyone. Have you reviewed it lately?"

"No, I haven't," she answered, remembering how her grandparents had shieled her from watching the news, stripping her of a chance to see footage of anything pertaining to her parents' deaths, though she was able to pull up several newspapers clippings on them years later.

"I'm sorry!" Hendrix offered. "I didn't mean to stir up old feelings."

"It's okay," she said as the elevator reached their floor and they got off. "It's been almost twenty years. I think I'm pretty much in control of my feelings by now, but no, I haven't had the slightest interest in reliving that part of my past."

"That's understandable." They reached Ebony's office and stopped. "Will you be long? I mean, I just have to grab my briefcase and I'll be right back out."

"No, it's okay, Hendrix," Ebony told him, using her key to unlock her door. "I have to file some stuff away. Then, I have to have a chat with someone before I head out. I'll just see you in the morning."

"Well, I guess this is goodnight."

"It is. I'll see you tomorrow."

As Hendrix made for his office, Ebony entered hers and locked the door, wondering why he was being so nice to her after all the 'un-nice' comments she'd made towards him. Perhaps, he was trying to get on her good side Ebony concluded, placing her briefcase atop the desk before taking a seat behind it, where she sat as still as possible, listening for any and every sound beyond the door.

Upon being released for the day, Ebony had planned to head on out to the gym for her routine, but what Larry Hendrix revealed to her brought on a mental alteration of that plan. With her curiosity now piqued, Ebony knew that she could not exit the building sans taking a trip down to the basement first.

Now, hearing the jingling of keys, her eyes shot to the bottom of the door seconds before a shadow zipped by. Ebony waited patiently. Hearing the ding of the elevator and figuring it to be Hendrix on his way out, she quickly donned her coat, gathered her briefcase and pocketbook, then exited the office, making for the elevators. Regarding the digital numbers above, she saw that one of the two elevators was descending to the ground floor. She waited until it stopped on the ground floor before ringing for one. The other elevator was on the third floor, so it was the first to arrive.

Entering the shaft, Ebony pressed for the basement, then planted her back against the rear of it, hoping she'd make it to her destination in time. However, she was thankful that no stops were made as the cart finally reached the bottom of the building. As always Ebony strolled the hallway of the basement, it reminded her of hospital's mortuary with its dim lighting, off-white walls, and highly polished linoleum floor. Plus, there's always a faint mildew odor commingled with some kind of cleaning agent. Reaching the service desk, she saw that Officer Blake Towns was preparing to leave for the day.

"Leaving early, Mr. Towns?" she asked the young man who was in his mid-twenties, and of the same complexion as herself.

"Not really," he answered, revealing the gap between his fairly white teeth. "I'm just making sure that I have everything together so I can shoot out the door when the time comes. How are you?"

"I'm fine," Ebony told him. "How's marriage life treating you?"

"It's rough," the officer admitted. Slowly shaking his head with a smile on his face. "One minute, she has me feeling like the luckiest man on Earth. The next minute, she has me feeling like I've committed a crime and landed on probation. Don't tell her I said that though. So, what brings you to the dungeon at this time of day?"

"I need you to buzz me in."

"Sure," He slid the sign-in chart over to her. "You won't be long right?"

"Nope," She slid the chart back to him.

"Come on, Ms. Davis!" Towns voiced, pushing it back towards her. "You know you have to sign in to get clearance."

"Only if I want this visit to go on record," she stated slowly, locking eyes with him. "And this visit is not going on record."

Officer Towns looked genuinely addled. "It's not?"

"Of course not," she pushed the chart back across the desk for the last time. "Kind of like your drug habit."

"I don't have a drug habit," he went into defense mode.

"Blake," Ebony spoke as if addressing a small child. "It's easy to say that when the only drug test requires for this job is prior to getting it. Any additional drug testing will result from a superior becoming suspicious of their subordinate. Perhaps, an anonymous tip would do the trick."

Blake Towns seemed at a loss for words.

"Smart man!" she prompted. "If you keep this visit between us, nobody'll know about your ventures to University Street, to get your fix, which could also affect Charles. He is your supplier right?"

The look on the young officer's face was nothing short of disbelief, which brought a huge smile to Ebony's face. She didn't want to play this card with him, but he forced her hand. Had he not been trying to play 'super cop', she would have never revealed to him that she was aware of him purchasing crush from one of her workers on a regular basis.

"Oh, well." she thought as she moved to the steel door beside the booth. There was nothing more left to say. Either he was going to press the button that released the locks on the door or call her bluff. Ebony seriously doubted if he would...

Click!

Without a second of hesitation nor a glance in Town's direction, Ebony pushed the steel door open and entered the room that boasted a temperature analogous to that of a mortuary, being that it wasn't equipped with any kind of heating or air controlling system. She hoped to be there no longer than a few minutes, figuring what she was looking for wouldn't be too hard to find.

The heavy steel door slammed shut behind Ebony, startling her a little. As she moved amid the numerous metal shelves containing any and every kind of evidence, she focused her attention on their gold-plated labels that categorized them by year. This was a good thing because she was able to follow their pattern until she came upon the shelf that was marked '2005'.

Feeling as if she was finally close, Ebony searched the label of every box and bag for the appellation of Carlos West, the man responsible for the demise if her father. But, to her dismay, there was not one item with his name on it. That's when it dawned in her that all evidence pertaining to Carlos West's case had been shipped to the GBI's evidence warehouse in Atlanta, being that West is deceased, which automatically closed the case, but Hendrix claimed that he'd just reviewed the footage if her father's murder, today. So, surely, it couldn't have been shipped out today. She was tempted to question officer Towns, but thought against it, figuring she'd browse around for another minute or so.

As she did, she came upon a metal cabinet that stood at about six feet. Looking at the keyhole in its handle, Ebony assumed it was lock. She would have repudiated it, had '*PROPERTY OF LINKTON COUNTY COURTHOUSE*' not been boldly displayed on it in crimson paint. With her free hand, she turned the handle and pulled one of the double doors open on its hinges. After swinging the other one open, Ebony stood there, eyeing the contents.

The shelves contained various boxes, bags, and manila envelopes, neatly stacked in their own piles, which made it easy for her to spot the manila envelope on top with '*Tyrone T. Davis*' above '*June 15, 2005.*' Ebony immediately took hod of it and felt the DVD case move around freely inside. With the content confirmed, she didn't see any need to open the envelope. Therefore, she stuffed it inside her pocketbook, then made for the exit. Towns buzzed her out and seemed to still have the same puzzled look on his face.

"I'm glad we were able to come to an agreement, Mr. Towns," Ebony said upon returning to the desk. "I was unsuccessful in finding what I was searching for, but I appreciate your time. However, you still haven't seen me, right?"

"Right," he answered with a slight nod of his head.

"You're one of a kind, Blake!"

With that, Ebony made for the elevators calling up the options on her cellular to start her car, so the console was nice and warm when she climbed in behind the wheel. Placing her things on the front passenger seat, she retrieved her second phone and dialed Rick's number.

"I'm listening," his voice came through on the other end.

"Are you busy?" Ebony wanted to know.

"Would it matter if I was?" The acerbity in his tone was thick.

"Not really," she shot back, with authority. "I need you to find one of those ancient DVD players and meet me back at my place, pronto!"

Ebony rung off before he could respond, though she doubted he had anything to say. Stuffing the phone back into her pocketbook, Ebony drove out of the parking garage, thankful that she didn't encounter Samantha on her way out. Right now, she had too much on her mind to be cordial, which was why she was taking a rain check on her visit to the gym today. She figured that she would take a shower and wait patiently for Rick to arrive, but his car was already parked in front of her house when she got there. He wasn't inside the car, so Ebony figured he let himself into her home.

Upon entering, Ebony encountered Rick seated on the living room sofa, sporting a pair of dark sunglasses, with one leg rested on the other. She couldn't see his eyes, but she could tell that he was preoccupied by what was playing on the television mounted on the wall. She turned to look at the screen. The movie playing wasn't familiar, but she recognized the black box sitting on the floor with the thick, black cord running from it to the back of the TV set.

"I can't believe you still own one of those," Ebony said, placing her pocketbook and briefcase on the coffee table.

"I don't just throw away stuff because they've upgraded," Rick responded, still watching the screen.

"And what's this movie?"

"Alex Cross," he answered, "I think Tyler Perry did a good job as the lead actor."

"I'm quite sure," she replied, taking off her coat, and tossing it onto the recliner. "However, I need to interrupt your program for a moment."

Rick didn't reply. Ebony pulled the manila envelope from her pocketbook and extracted the clear DVD case. The disc had '*ADA Tyrone Davis: 6-15-05*' written on it in black marker. Despite how she was feeling, while switching the discs, Ebony didn't pass up the chance to entice the older man by parting her legs slightly as she bent down to do so. Once this was complete, she straightened her posture, then turned to face him, looking for any sign of interest. His facial expression was immutable, and she still couldn't see his eyes for those damn sunglasses.

"Perhaps, he's not interested in women," she thought, placing the ejected disc onto the coffee table which was where she retrieved the remote control from. Pressing Play, she sat down in the recliner, not bothering to remove her coat. Her stunt may not have been enough to turn Rick on, but she was definitely affected by it. This had he wondering if she could come up with a way to threaten, or blackmail him into having sex with her.

Ebony's prurient thoughts were encroached by the image that flashed onto screen. She'd seen a handful of her father's publicized trials when she was a child, but this single camera view of him in the courtroom was bizarre to her. She didn't expect the picture to be in color, but it was. In this particular feature, Ebony saw her father sitting at the State's table with a female prosecutor, whose name Ebony memorized as Michelle Johnson. The two of them seemed to be going over some documents. There was no one seated at the defense table, but a small amount of people were seated in the visitor's area. The stenographer was setting up her machine, and the bailiff was seated in the chair of the witness stand adjoined to the judge's bench, which was unoccupied.

For some reason, Ebony expected to see Carlos West barge into the courtroom at any moment, attack the bailiff with an ink pen, disarm him, then turn the gun on her father, but nothing happened for the next couple of minutes. Then Judge Dennis Lathan emerged from his chambers, minus his black robe. Instead of taking a seat in his chair, he stood behind it with both hands gripping the back of it and addressed those in attendance. Though Ebony couldn't read his visage correctly for the distant view of the camera, she got the notion that he was in a state of discontentment and was possibly handling down some troubling news. Then, suddenly, he disappeared back inside his chambers, which addled Ebony, who continued watching, thinking Carlos was going to burst through the doors at any second. But the only moment going on was that of the people seated in the visitors' area. They were now exiting the courtroom. She saw that her father and Michelle Johnson had gotten to their feet subsequently exiting alongside the court reporter, who didn't bother to disassemble her machine. This cause Ebony to regard the date and time displayed at the bottom of the screen. Though it showed the date as June 15, 2005, and the time as 8:47AM, it still didn't sit well with her. Something wasn't right.

"What the hell just happened?" Ebony inquired, now regarding the older man, who was still looking at the television. "Either that time is wrong, or it's a bit too early for quitting time."

"It's not wrong," Rick told her, now looking in her direction. "You'll have to fast forward it. The incident happened sometime after two."

Ebony fast-forward the disc until the first sign of life reappeared on the screen, which were the bailiff and court reporter. The time on the screen was 1:43PM Nearly two minutes had gone by when assistant D.A.'s Tyrone Davis, and Michelle Johnson, re-entered, taking their seats. Periodically. Somebody would saunter in and sit in the visitor's area, but Ebony intently watched her father, now realizing that she was witnessing him in his last moments of his natural existence.

At 1:53, a well-dressed Caucasian male, carrying a briefcase entered the courtroom, and stopped by the State's table to shake hands and conversate with Tyrone. After the laconic encounter, the man approached the defense table, and begun pulling documents from his briefcase before sitting it on the floor, and taking a seat in one of the two chairs, He then turned and spoke to a male visitor who was accompanied by a woman, seconds before Judge Lathan emerged from his chambers, and bid everyone to remain seated while taking his own. He addressed the courtroom then apparently sent the court officer to retrieve an inmate from the holding cells. At this time Ebony's eyes were glued to the side door that the officer went through. To her, it seemed to have taken forever before he returned with a black male inmate, clad in an orange jumpsuit, and hands cuffed in front of him. Carlos West's face was burned into her memory years ago, so there was no mistaking the man she was glaring angrily at.

Once the bailiff removed the manacles, Carlos seemed to look about the room, prior to taking a seat beside his attorney. Then, the motion for a new trial begins with the attorney getting to his feet to present an argument. In conclusion, he bowed slightly then re-took his seat. Tyrone stood and purveyed the court with his reasons for why the motion should be denied. When he sat down, Ebony shifted her gaze to the judge, knowing it was now on him to make his very own decision in the matter.

When the judge began speaking, Ebony was once again studying Carlos West's every move. Judge Lathan must've asked if West had anything to say because he shook his head. This Ebony knew was the moment for the judge's final ruling, which was the denying of the motion. As the bailiff stepped forward to reapply the handcuffs, she saw West furtively take possession of what appeared to be an ink pen before slowly getting to his feet. Then like some stuntman in an action movie, Carlos wheeled on the officer with exceptional speed, jamming the pen into his neck. The officer stumbled backwards, gagging, but before he could tumble to the floor, Carlos commandeered the gun from the holster with ease. At this time, on instinct, everybody else in the room threw themselves to the floor except for Tyrome, who endeavored to make a break for the exit. Carlos had again spun on his heels with the same blinding speed. Though the video was inaudible, Ebony felt she could hear the report as she saw sparks emitted from the barrel of the gun, three times. The slugs impacted her father's body forcing him to the floor. Then Carlos quick-stepped over him, gun still aimed. Slowly Tyrone turned onto his back, revealing what appeared to be blood oozing from his mouth while clutching his side. He seemed to be talking to the gunman, but Ebony found it hard to believe he was pleading for his life.

Suddenly one if the female visitors got up off the floor and took over the conversation. She and Carlos spoke briefly just before a white male court officer barged in with his weapon at the ready, stopping several feet away from Tyrone's head. This is where Ebony became really confused. She expected for the officer to take immediate action, but he seemed to be trying to negotiate with the armed criminal instead. She could clearly see her father urging him to do away with the imminent threat. The standing woman, whom Ebony deduced was the responsible for Carlos West's incarceration, appeared to be trying to talk him out of getting himself killed. Then. That's when it happened. With the gun still aimed at Tyron, Carlos squeezed the trigger sending a fatal shot to his head. Then he quickly raised the gun at the responding officer, but the officer reacted much faster, firing off a succession of rounds, knocking Carlos backwards to the floor, where he ultimately expired. Now, extremely livid, ebony turned to Rick, who was still watching the screen.

"He could've prevented that shit!" she asserted through clenched teeth.

Rick looked at her but said nothing.

"He actually stood there and let my father get murdered," Ebony resumes in the same tone. "That makes him equally responsible."

"Frank Mann," Rick finally spoke.

"Do we have a location on him?"

"We will once you look him up tomorrow," he told her. "And I'll make sure to have Bull on standby."

"All I need is you," Ebony replied. "Just be ready to go when I call."

Chapter 5

The loud ringing of the phone beside the bed roused Anthony from his sleep. As if that wasn't enough, the bright sun rays filtering through the thin curtains assaulted his eyes the moment he opened them. Closing them back, he blindly reached over for the phone, pulling the receiver from its cradle.

"Hello?" he groggily whispered into the mouthpiece.

"Good morning, sir!" a female's voice breached his ear in a high pitch. "This is your ten o'clock wake-up call as requested.

"Yeah, thank you!" he said, then slammed the receiver into the cradle before she could tell him that he was welcome, or ask if he needed any other assistance.

Finally forcing his eyes open to accept the momentary discomfort, Anthony stretched his limbs for a few seconds before sitting up, swinging his legs over the side of the bed, and sliding his feet into the soft soles of his house shoes. It didn't take long for his eyes to find bearings. In a pair of pajama pants and a white tank top that accentuated his muscular physique, he plodded across the room to the bathroom where he drained his aching bladder prior to brushing his teeth.

Anthony had checked into Windham hotel in Warner Robins upon leaving Atlanta, Georgia on Monday, and had been lying low since then contemplating his next move. He was running low on cash and knew that he had to drive out to his home in Macon. The drive was inevitable, but Anthony also knew that he had to move with extreme caution being that war has officially been declared between him and Ebony, and she incontestably had the upper hand, considering she was a crime boss with hired goons. He was all alone with no allies. Plus, he was pretty sure that she was cognizant of what had happened to her henchman on Saturday, and probably had others stationed outside his house, assuming he'd eventually return for whatever reason. Had it not been for the fact that he was almost out of money and needed to get to the stash inside his home, he wouldn't be anywhere near Macon right now.

Upon leaving the hotel, minutes after eleven, Anthony drove out to the nearest vehicle rental store and traded his car in for a burgundy Honda Accord, hoping it was inconspicuous enough for him to blend in, and get what he needed to get done. Leaving there, he drove out to Linkton County Health Department.

In the parking lot Anthony removes his skullcap and gander at himself in the rearview mirror. The dark-framed, non-medicated eyeglasses on his face gave him an intelligent edge, although he was wearing them more for somewhat of a disguise feature. He just wished that he could carry the 9mm inside with him, being that he didn't know who or what would be waiting for him when he exited the establishment. He's already disposed of the P.98 sub-machine gun, so the handgun was all he had until he was able to get to the ones at his house.

Shutting off the engine, Anthony grabbed the manila folder off the front passenger seat, and dismounted, looking about the parking lot, while pretending to brush lint from his green suit. Not noticing anything out of the ordinary, he crossed the lot thankful that the wind seemed to become less intense as the month grew shorter.

"Hello, sir!" the female receptionist at the front desk greeted him. "How may I help you?"

"I'm here to see a Dr. Shannon," Anthony replied, noticing the air conditioner didn't make the interior feel any better than how it felt beyond the front doors.

"Which one?"

"Which one!" Anthony had a confused look on his face.

"How many are there?"

"Two," she answered, an amused smirk on her face. "They're husband and wife."

"Well, I guess I'm here to see the husband."

Now, her smirk turned into a mock frown. "I hate to be the bearer of bad news," she said, "but Mr. Shannon will be out until next Monday."

"Is it possible that I could speak briefly with the missus?"

"Did you have an appointment with Mr. Shannon?" the woman wanted to know. "I mean. I'm quite sure that I've called and rescheduled every appointment he had for this week."

"I didn't have an appointment," Anthony admitted, hoping he didn't have to leave without acquiring some kind of information. "But I really do need to speak with Mrs. Shannon. It's important."

"Is it a matter of life or death?"

He didn't reply.

"What is your name?" she asked, taking hold of the desk's phone receiver.

"Anthony Hudson."

The receptionist dialed four digits, waited a moment, then spoke into the phone, "Yes, Mrs. Shannon? I know you're busy, but I am with Mr. Anthony Hudson who claims he needs to speak to you about an important matter... No, ma'am. I'll relay the message."

She hung up the phone then regarded Anthony. "She'll see you, but you'll have to wait until she finishes with her patients."

"That's fair enough," Anthony offered gratefully.

"Great!" the woman expressed, smiling broadly. "She's located on the second floor, Waiting Room Two."

Anthony made for the elevators, casting furtive glances at any and everyone coming into his line of sight. The elevators he got onto was packed mainly with women and children, as well people. Anthony knew that he was in for a very long wait, but he figured it wouldn't be as bad if his ears didn't have to suffer the perpetual screams and wailing of the small children. Then he was sure that other people were set to show up between then and five o'clock, which had him wondering just how long he'd be waiting.

***

"How much longer do you have before you graduate from prosecuting jay walkers and drunk drivers?" Samantha asked Roselyn Holt, who was seated across the table from Ebony and herself.

"I'm giving it until March of next year," the state court prosecutor replied, taking a sip of her lemonade. "I mean, what I do is fun, and not as burdensome as what you guys do, but I'm in dire need of a payment increase. And maybe a change of venue."

"You're thinking about leaving Linkton?" Samantha seemed surprised.

"Shit, yeah!" exclaimed Holt. "I don't know what's going on around here, but Linkton County is no longer a place of euphoria."

"I totally agree with you in that," Samantha avowed in an almost conspiring tone. "It's not the violence I'm concerned with because it's everywhere. It's the fact that people are constantly being murdered, and nothing's being done about it. I was watching the news the other night, and they acknowledged that the violence hasn't been this significant since two thousand and five."

"That's nineteen years ago," Holt chimed in.

"Of course." Samantha turned to face Ebony. "Call me crazy, but I think I'm being stalked by some psychopathic killer, who's waiting for the right moment to make me a statistic."

"You're just being paranoid," said Ebony, whose mind has been elsewhere for the most part of the day. "It's okay to be a little spooked, but I think you're blowing it all out of proportion, Sam."

"Oh, you think?"

"There's a strong possibility." Ebony gander at her watch seeing that she had a little over thirty minutes left on her break time. "I hate to leave so soon, but I have to grab some things from my office before returning to the courtroom. I'll see you girls later."

"Okay," replied Holt.

Samantha didn't respond, which didn't matter to Ebony who's gotten up from the table and exited the cafeteria. She couldn't blame her friend for being a little paranoid, but Ebony, who was responsible for the spike in the murder rate in Linkton County knew for sure that Samantha Gordon had no reason to fear this psychopathic killer she'd conjured all of a sudden. Though Ebony claimed she had to stop by her office that was not the case. Truth be told, her destination was Records, which was on the same floor as the cafeteria. Ambling past the elevators, she approached the small, nondescript door that gave no indications as to what was beyond it and held the barcode of her identification card up to the reader. There was a beeping sound, supervened by the faint clicking of the lock.

Ebony pushed the knob less door open then entered the small room that was equipped with a desk and an array of file cabinets lining one wall. As if the windowless room wasn't enough to make her feel claustrophobic, the turquoise painted walls seemed to induce an immediate sense of dreariness. The whole setting made Ebony feel compassionate towards Elizabeth Whyte, the dark-haired woman seated behind the cluttered desk.

"Hi, Ebony!" Whyte exclaimed, her green eyes beaming beyond the clear lenses of the slightly large eyeglasses on her face.

"How's it going, Liz?" Ebony replied taking a seat in the metal folding chair before the desk.

"Everything is just going," she responded, placing her elbows on tip of the desk, and steepling her fingers. "How's Judge Jackson been treating you? Are you two still at each other's throats?"

"You know how it is in the courtroom," Ebony said, a plastered smile on her face. "Everything is political. It's all for show. Despite how it may be viewed by outsiders, Jackson and I are far from enemies."

"As heard from the horse's mouth," the woman who was a few years older than Ebony voiced. "So, what can I assist you with?"

"I was wondering if files were kept on former employees," Ebony answered. "And if so, how far back do they go?"

"Yes, files are kept on former employees," Elizabeth told her. "How far do they go back? Well, that depends on which file you're snooping through. The prehistoric scrolls are pretty much for decoration and would probably help you out when the computer's down for whatever reason, but don't count on it. However, the electronic file is the shit! It's accessible to the public and it automatically upgrades when addresses and phone numbers are changed. Plus, it goes back to the first person to ever walk through the front door of this building a hundred decades ago."

Ebony simpered. "Very funny, Liz!"

The woman shrugged he shoulders up and down. "That's just my illustration of how high proficient the electric file is. So, who should I pull up for you?"

"Frank Mann," Ebony answered. "M-A-N-N."

"Frank Mann," Whyte repeated, tapping keys on her computer's keyboard. "It doesn't ring a bell, but...Oh! That's why I never heard of him. He resigned in two thousand and five."

"Are you sure?" Ebony asked, wondering how she was going to acquire the address without tipping Whyte off.

"That's what it says here," Whyte turned the monitor in Ebony's direction.

Ebony had to fight the urge to jump across the desk and kiss the woman in the mouth for what she'd just done, but as she began to commit the address to memory, she realized that Whyte would be a valuable tool to the authorities once Mann is discovered. She had no doubt that Whyte would mention this visit to them, voluntarily, which was something she didn't think of before entering the office. So, yes Elizabeth Whyte had inadvertently sealed her fate.

Chapter 6

"Mr. Hudson?"

Anthony looked up from the outdated magazine that he was sifting aimlessly through at the sound of his name being called by the practical nurse, who'd been in and out of the service door summoning all scheduled clients for the past four hours he'd been in the waiting area. At this time, he realized that he was the only somebody left.

"I guess that would be me," Anthony said placing the magazine back onto the table with the others before getting to his feet and moving towards the young woman.

"She didn't believe you'd wait this long," the nurse informed as he approached. "Right this way sir."

Anthony followed the nurse through the corridor where other nurses bustled to and from as if preparing to leave for the day being that it was close to quitting time, but their journey was short. Stopping at one of the examination rooms where the door was standing wide open, the nurse stood aside and gestured for him to enter.

With the manila folder in tow, Anthony did just that. Dr. Shannon had her head down, scribbling something into a folder. Her dark hair was pulled into a ponytail that lingered at her upper back, accentuated by a bang resembling a spiral staircase that poised at the right side of her temple. She was beautiful an at least twenty years younger than the man he was searching for. After another moment of doodling, she looked up, giving Anthony a once-over before regarding the nurse, who was still standing just outside the door.

"Thanks, Tiller!" she told the younger woman. "I'll see you in the morning."

"Yes, ma'am!"

"And I assume you're Anthony Hudson?" Dr. Shannon said, once the nurse had gone.

"I am," he answered. "And thanks for seeing me on such a short notice."

"No problem," She gestured to the chair before her. Once Anthony had taken a seat, she asked: "So, how may I help you?"

"Last year," he started, "on the fifth of July, I received a visit from a Dr. Shannon. That would be your husband, right?"

"Well," she replied, closing the folder in front of her, "I am married to a Dr. Shannon. He visited you at your home?"

"He visited me in jail," Anthony said studying her for any sign of apprehension, in which he didn't receive.

He would've lied about the location, but figured the truth would come out once she brought this visit to her husband's attention.

"Did it have anything to do with Child Services?" Shannon asked, clearly accustomed to being in the presence of ex-criminals.

"No," he answered, handing the folder across the desk to her. "But it was pertaining to a DNA testing."

"Ancestral DNA testing," she said, studying the sole document in front of her. "This is a very tricky procedure in which only certified medical personnel are allowed to conduct."

"Are you certified?"

"As of January."

"What about Mr. Shannon?"

"He was one of the first to be cleared for the procedure," she answered then narrowed her eyes at him. "Are you having reservations about your results?"

"Yes, I am."

"After all this time?"

"I don't think it's accurate."

Slowly closing the folder in front of her, Dr. Shannon leaned back in her chair with an incredulous look on her face. "And what caused you to draw this inference all of a sudden?"

"A lot of things," Anthony answered with a sigh. "Too much to go into, in fact."

"So, what is it that you're asking of me?"

"To re-do the test."

"As if I dissent with the findings of every analyst that partook in that procedure?" she asked, as if such a thing could be considered treason.

"There were more than one?"

"There's always more than one," the doctor informed. "Each procedure undergoes two tests by two different analysts before being inspected by a panel approval."

"Does that mean I can't have the test re-done?"

"You can have the test re-done as many times as you like," she told him. "You'll just have to schedule an appointment, and make sure that all parties are present."

"All parties?" Anthony was confused.

"Everyone who was required to give DNA for the first procedure," she clarified. "In your case, there's another person by the name of Ebony Davis. Just make sure that she's present."

Damn! Anthony swore mentally. Scheduling and making the appointment wouldn't be much a problem, but he knew that there was no way he could get Ebony there alive. But what if he could have Dr. Shannon lure her in on a separate appointment with the pretext that the clinic has upgraded its software, and needed a fresh DNA sample from her? Surely, that would work.

"Is everything all right?" Dr. Shannon posed, apparently considering his delay of response.

"Huh? Yeah?" he answered, breaking from his reverie. He then reached over and opened the folder back up on the desk. "Dr. Shannon, suppose I have a suspicion that this document has been altered?"

***

It seemed as though every judge at the Linkton County courthouse had adjourned at the same time, whereas a majority of the prosecutors managed to exit the building together, headed for their respective vehicles. Being that Larry Hendrix had insisted on walking Samantha out to her car, he was still in the company of she and Ebony.

"I thought National Breast Cancer Awareness Month was September," Hendrix said, conducing to the conversation that Ebony and Samantha sparked about a dinner at the governor's mansion.

"October," Samantha corrected. "But Governor Spires always throws a dinner party for Dorthy Stockholm in March, being that it's the only time of the year she's in Georgia."

"And you two are friends with the governor?" he queried.

Samantha and Ebony exchanged glances, but Ebony took the initiative.

"I guess you could say that. We ended up on his guess list from time to time."

"That's great!" Hendrix exclaimed. "Hell, I've been in Atlanta forever, and I still don't know what the mansion looks like."

"Outdone by a couple of hillbillies, huh?" Ebony said as they approached her car and stopped.

"Ebony!" Samantha chided, shooting a sideways glance at her friend.

"What?"

"Stop it!"

Ebony put on her innocent façade. Stop what, Sam?"

Samantha narrowed her eyes. "You promised."

"And I always keep my promised." Ebony disarmed her alarm and pulled the driver's door open. "I'll see you two in the morning."

"Goodnight!" said Hendrix.

"I'll call you later, girl," Samantha told her.

They moved on as Ebony climbed into her car. While waiting for the engine to warm up, she fished her pre-paid cellular from the glove compartment and pulled Rick's number. Some ancient rhythm and blues song seemed to play on endlessly, before his pleasant-sounding voice impregnated her eardrum, causing her heart to flutter.

"I'm listening," he said upon answering.

"I got the address," she appraised, "but there's one slight problem."

"And what's that?"

"The receptionist in Records," Ebony relayed. "She had to pull Mann up for me in order for me to acquire the information, although I memorized it without tipping her off to what I was up to."

"So, she has to be eliminated," Rick said obviously realizing how critical it would be to allow Elizabeth Whyte to exist longer than necessary.

"Of course," Ebony coincided not missing a beat. And for some reason, she didn't feel a bit remorseful about what she agreed to.

Chapter 7

The unmarked, police issued car had been parked across the street from the green house since 8:37PM Now or was almost ten o'clock, and there had been no sign of inhabitation within the place, although there was an older model Ford SUV sitting in its driveway. The curtains in its windows were made of thick material, which only allowed for a small portion of light to be seen by the casual observer. On the outside of the house, the only movement was that of some residents returning home from their daily activities. Other than that, the neighborhood was relatively quiet.

"How much longer do you suppose we wait?" asked Ebony who was seated in the back seat, clad in black jeans under her black trench coat with her hair wrapped and tucked inside of a black skull cap, and her gloved hands rested in her lap.

"That's your call," Rick said from the driver's seat keeping his eyes on the house.

"Well, thanks for the confirmation, Rick!" she sassed, shooting daggers at the back of his head though she was sitting directly behind the front passenger seat. "In fact, I think now would be the perfect time to exploit your electronics skills. And we're using the back door. Once everything is in order, you know where to find us.

She watched as Rick exited and ambled across the street as if he was part of the residency, clad in a black trench coat and skullcap. With his shoulders hunched and his hands tucked into the pockets of his coat, he moved along the side of the house towards the back as casually as someone set out to reset the fuse processor. Then he was out of sight.

"I placed that order with Napoleon," Bull said from the front passenger seat, pulling Ebony from abstract musing. "He said everything's a go, but he'll contact us whenever he can set a proper date."

"That's fine," she replied, still watching the house for any sign of movement.

Besides the humming of the car's engine there was a long period of silence before Bull asked: "Have you considered finding someone else to take Anthony's place?"

"I have," Ebony answered.

"I think Rick and I have the perfect candidate."

She was now looking at the back of the headrest of the seat that he was in. "You think?"

"Well," he started, sifting in his seat. "We've considered one of our workers but, of course, you have the final say so."

A smile slowly creased her face. "You seem quite anxious to get from under my employment, Bull. Do I not pay well?"

"The pay is good", he admitted. "I'm just trying to fulfill my part of the agreement."

"To free yourself of obligations, huh?"

Bull remained silent.

"I guess you're wondering if I'm gonna keep my word and let you and rick go without accident, right?"

He was still silent.

"Of course," she went on, making the form of a gun with one of her gloved hands, pointing at the back of his head and pretending to shoot him while mouthing, *"Pow."* "I always keep my word."

At that time, movement caught from the corners of her eyes, drew Ebony's attention back to the house across the street. Rick was standing on the side of it, beckoning for them to join him. Bull, who also saw him, cut the car off, but left the keys in the ignition. Then he finally turned to look back at Ebony.

"It's on us," he said.

Without another word spoken between the two, Ebony and Bull dismounted, and crossed the street just as casual as Rick had done. Once they reached him, Rick turned on his heels, and led the way to the back door that appeared unmolested.

"Shall we?" Rick asked, drawing his gun, prompting Bull to follow suit.

Without waiting for a response, he grabbed the knob with his free gloved hand, and eased the door open. As they entered directly into the well-lit kitchen, with Ebony bringing up the rear, they all paused to listen out for any sound of movement while Ebony quietly shut the door behind her.

After a few seconds of only hearing the sound of a television playing somewhere in a distance, Ricky, with his gun at the ready, led the way making it to the doorway of a bedroom. He paused long enough to peer inside then moved along. Ebony assumed the room was unoccupied but didn't know for sure until she passed it herself.

The sound of the television grew louder as they neared the living room where they came to a halt at the threshold. After peering in, Rick held one finger up, then gestured for them to stay put. Then he walked past the living room, ostensibly to comb the rest of the house, leaving Ebony wondering if that one finger meant that Frank Mann was alone. She wanted to take a look but was blocked by Bull who took the initiative to do so.

Momentarily, Rick returned, positioning himself on the opposite side of the living room's threshold. He exchanged a look with Bull before looking past him to Ebony who was regarding him with expectant eyes.

"He's alone," Rick said, in a hushed tone. "Are you ready?"

Ebony nodded.

Not wasting another second, Rick marched into the living room supervened by Bull. Ebony rounded the corner just in time to catch a glimpse of the older man before Rick brought the butt of his gun down on the top of his head from behind, knocking him out of the dilapidated recliner he occupied. He cried out in pain, holding the impacted area with both hands while folding himself into a fetal position.

"Shut up!" Bull scolded, delivering a kick to the injured man's abdomen causing him more pain, though he did his best to muffle his cries.

Ebony joined Bull now standing a few feet away from Frank Mann's head while Rick commenced to connect the portable DVD player he'd brought to the television mounted to the wall. She re-directed her attention back to Mann, who had apparently gotten over his pain and was now looking around at them wide-eyed still maintaining the fetal position.

"On your back, Frank!" Ebony commanded. "Ther's something I want you to see. And I want you to pay close attention because I also have a few questions for you."

Slowly, he rolled onto his back placing his arms at his sides, and gave Ebony and Bull another once-over, before looking over to Rick, who was still wrestling with the wires. That's when Ebony was able to get a better look at the man, who was clearly 19 years older than herself, and bared no resemblance to the man she's seen in the video, being that he'd gained a great deal of weight, and was now completely bald at the top with fine gray hairs rounding the sides and back of his head. He was unshaven so these same-colored hairs pretty much obscured the lower part of his face. He had on a pair of dingy, faded jeans, and a gray sweater that did little to hide his bulging stomach. Aside from disgust, the hatred for Frank Mann was now stirring inside of her like a category five hurricane, and he was definitely going to get caught up in its rapture.

"All set," Rick promulgated, once he was done.

"Pay close attention, Mr. Mann!" Ebony said, then nodded to Rick who activated the portable DVD player.

When the image of the courtroom appeared on the screen, Ebony looked down at Frank Mann, whose visage then conveyed apprehension as if he was watching a horror film, indicating that he was well aware of the reason for this abrupt visit. Then he slowly lifted his frightened eyes to meet hers.

"I asked you to pay close attention to the screen, Frank," Ebony spoke as if to a child.

"Y-you're Ebony Davis," he stammered, recognition registering in his eyes.

"The screen, Frank!" she told him, now annoyed at the fact that he deprived her of the pleasure of introducing herself.

The old man's gaze lingered on a little longer before reverting to the screen. Ebony also turned her attention back to the television. At this time, Judge Lathan had entered the courtroom, sans his robe, and addressed the people in attendance.

"Fast-forward it!" she told Rick.

Doing as he was instructed, Rick moved the video along, only to resume at the part where the bailiff and court reporter re-entered the courtroom, following the five hour long recess. Just as she'd done on her first time viewing the video, Ebony's eyes were on her father from the moment he entered up until Carlos West came into the picture. She didn't peel her eyes away from the screen until Frank Mann rushed into the courtroom with his service weapon drawn, and her now wounded father was lying on the ground, staring down the barrel of the gun that Carlos West had taken from the appointed court officer. Looking down at Mann, she saw that he was visibly perspiring, and his breathing had become labored, which they could hear, being that the video had no sound.

"This is the part that addles me, Frank," Ebony spoke garnering his attention. "Being that there's no sound, I'm gonna need you to assist me. Look at the screen1"

Reluctantly, he did as he was told.

"Now," she continued, "at this point, there's an exchange going on between you and my father. Translate!"

Frank Mann cleared his throat before asserting: "I was instructing Carlos West to drop the weapon, which is what I was trained to do in such situations, but your father was egging me to take him down. Again, I instructed West to surrender his weapon."

"So, you pretty much ignored my father's plea for help," Ebony stated watching Carlos West deliver the fatal shot before Mann finally decided to eliminate the threat that was no longer a threat to the one she cared about. "But you did manage to save yourself, huh?"

"I acted completely on impulse," Mann begged to differ, drilling his pleading eyes into hers. "My first priority was to keep them both alive."

"Bullshit!" Ebony spat nodding to Bull, who responded by brandishing a black revolver, in which he began screwing a silencer onto the barrel of. "Your first priority was to preserve my father's life, which you failed to do. However, you were smart. You knew that the Board of Operations and Standards was going to penalize you for your actions, so you resigned. After all these years, you thought that you got away huh?"

The olde man visibly swallowed but said nothing.

"Get in position, Bull!" she barked.

As prearranged, Bull stepped closer and stood over Mann, the same exact way that Carlos West had stood over Tyrone Davis in his final moments making sire to aim the revolver at the former court officer's head.

"You're not begging for your life, Frank," Ebony acknowledged. "Do you not wish to live?"

"It doesn't matter what I wish, Ms. Davis," he finally spoke in a composed tone. "I'm quite sure you didn't go to all this trouble just to spare my life. Like I said, my intention was to keep them both alive. Other than that, I have nothing more to say."

With that the older man closed his eyes, pretty much accepting his fate, which was not how Ebony expected it to go. However, she couldn't force the ancient old fart to beg for his worthless life, right? Taking it for what it's worth, Ebony waved a dismissive hand at Bull, turned on her heels, then made for the entrance of the living room, making sure to be well out of the way of any DNA that may splatter about.

Bull didn't hesitate to execute. Though Ebony didn't look back and the gun wasn't loud due to the attached silencer, she could tell that three slugs were injected into Frank Mann's skull ending his very existence. But at that very moment, Ebony didn't feel any better. Liquidating Mann didn't bring her father back, but it was a start. Now, it was time for Rick and Bull to come clean with some answers on the death of her mother.

***

It was dark out when Anthony pulled the Honda Accord onto Heard Street. Had it not been for the extensive tract of forestry behind his home, he would have accessed a back street to enter his house that was purchased by Ebony, who has her own keys to get in with, and knew the passcode to the alarm system. For this matter, he figured she had goons watching his abode, if they were not already inside awaiting his arrival, though nobody knew he was returning tonight.

Before pulling into his driveway, Anthony visibly searched the semi-dark street for anyone who could be occupying any of the several vehicles that were present. Seeing nothing out of the ordinary, he parked, killed the engine, and quickly exited, stuffing the 9mm into a pocket on his coat. Gripping the weapon with his left hand, he used his keys to negotiate the security locks before gingerly easing the door open to total darkness. The only light he could see was the tiny one blinking on the alarm box that was pretty much letting him know that he only had seconds to punch in the code of acknowledgement, before the Bibb County Police Department receives a signal that would indicate that a possible break-in was in progress.

After closing the front door, and ensconcing himself into more darkness, Anthony quickly typed in the code, then drew his gun, holding it close to his chest with the barrel pointed while setting his feet into motion. Feeling as though he could maneuver through the house, blindfolded, Anthony listened intently as he cautiously crossed the threshold onto the living room, gracefully sweeping the barrel back and forth. Seeing nothing out of place, he eased back int the small hallway making for the first of the three bedrooms.

Once he cleared that room, which only contained clothing that wouldn't fit into the closet of his bedroom, he only peered into the bathroom that contained the only active light, though the door was pulled up. Making sure to extinguish the light, and pull the door back closed, Anthony searched the final two bedrooms before going into the kitchen, where he analyzed the security locks on the back door to make sure that they hadn't been breached.

Seeing that the door was unmolested, and that no one was lying in wait for him, Anthony tucked his gun, while retracing his steps back to the main bedroom. Only using the meager light pouring in from the windows of the room, he first, retrieved a gray gym bag from the closet, tossing it onto the bed. Then he pulled the bed away from the wall.

Just beyond the headboard, there was a secret compartment built into the wall. It would take a person with a keen eye to spy the breach in it that blended in with the professionally layered white paint. Anthony pressed down on the button, which caused the hidden door to jut outwards.

Entering he felt blindly around for the chain overhead and pulled it, illuminating the small room with the sole lightbulb. Lining one side, was a wooden structure that had an assortment of assault rifles hanging up and several handguns running along the flat surface of it. As Anthony stood there, eyeing his collection, he began mentally formulating his plan of action, which entailed, first getting rid of Bull and Rick. Then once he puts Ebony in the ground, he would continue his search for Marvin, and get even with Janelle, or maybe, he should push Ebony's name to the top of his list.

Chapter 8

The following morning, at approximately 7:31AM, Elizabeth Whyte was exiting her apartment on her way to the Linkton County Courthouse, where she works in the Records Department. Tightening the waist belt of her cream-colored leather coat, Elizabeth crossed the parking lot to her white Infinity, deactivating the alarm. Upon climbing behind the wheel and starting the engine, she rubbed her hands together for warmth, while waiting for the console to warm up. Then suddenly, the driver's door was snatched open starling her. Before she could make any sense of what was going on, a man with a ski mask over his head filled the doorway with his huge frame, although Elizabeth was more focused on his large, gloved hands that immediately clamped around her neck and began squeezing. Her fight or flight instincts couldn't come fast enough. While it felt like her larynx was being crushed in by the second, Elizabeth reached her right hand out and bared down on the horn, blaring it. However, this didn't take long because just as quickly as she pressed it, a hand come from somewhere behind her assailant, grabbing her hand and bending it back with apparent intent to inflict pain. Well, this tact worked, but Elizabeth screamed was squelched from being strangled. As her lungs burned from deprivation of air, and tears cascaded down her face, she stared into the dark eyes of her murderer, wishing that she could latch her soul onto his and take him to hell with her, but that wasn't the case. When darkness finally overtook her, and she breathed her last breath, she found her soul floating towards that supernatural light all alone.

***

"You wanted to see me?" Ebony inquired upon sticking her head inside the office of Barbara Hutchins, who was seated behind her desk, with her the phone receiver up to her ear.

When Ebony arrived at her own office that morning, the first thing she noticed was the red indicator on her phone, indicating that she had messages. Figuring that one was from the Banner and Associates law firm in Texas, she deposited her things atop her desk, took a seat, then pushed the playback button. Though there was only a message, it wasn't from the law firm, but from the head district attorney, who claimed that she needed to see Ebony as soon as possible.

Now with the receiver still glued to her face, Barbara Hutchins waved her in, but kept talking as Ebony entered the room that reeked of the district attorney's awful smelling perfume that was probably manufactured back in the 1950's. However, Ebony tried her best not to make a face as she took a seat across from her supervisor.

"You'll have to sign keys out to Humphries," the head D.A. was saying into the receiver. "Don't worry, I'll all the front desk. By the time you get there, they'll be ready for you. Once you get Whyte's information, ring my line. I'll place the call."

Dropping the receiver into its cradle she looked over at Ebony.

"Elizabeth hasn't shown up to work yet. I can't even remember a time when she'd taken a day off or called in complaining of some kind of ailment. The older woman sighed. "Well, it's good to see that you check your messages when you get in."

Ebony didn't respond. Elizabeth Whyte's absence only meant that her men had succeeded in tying up their lose ends.

"Anyway," Hutchins resumed grabbing a manila folder off her desk handling it across to Ebony. "We have another change of venue case from Telfair County. Murder."

"And you've decided to give it to me," Ebony offered, accepting the folder. "What about Larry Hendrix? Don't you want…"

"No, I do not," Hutchins cut her off. "According to his resume, he's a great prosecutor, but I wouldn't dare put him up against Scarlatti, just yet."

"Scarlatti!" Ebony exclaimed almost lunging from her seat.

The last time that Ebony had encountered the Italian attorney was over 7 months ago when the two of then battled it out in a trial that Ebony is still a bit sore about losing, although Rebecca Scarlatti has a track record with a 97% success rate. Then at that instance, Ebony began to feel like the older woman was setting her up for failure. It didn't matter what kind of case was being brought forth. Hutchins had personal reasons to believe that Scarlatti would triumph and wanted to spare Hendrix the scars that the attorney would leave on his reputation. Though her suspicion may not reign true, Ebony intended to carry on as if that was the case.

"She's the counsel for the defendant," Hutchins now relayed. "In fact, she's the one who filed and got the change of venue motion granted, which rarely happens in Telfair County; especially with Judge Reese."

"Well, I'll look through it when I get the chance," Ebony promised, getting to her feet.

"You may want to look through it tonight," the head prosecutor advised. "As I was told, Scarlatti's already filing a motion for a speedy trial. And you already know how big of an influence she has on our judges."

***

Last night after collecting guns and money from his home, Anthony left back out as cautiously as he'd arrived and made it safely back to the hotel. Following a bout of unrest, he pulled himself out of bed with a mountain of pre-meditated thoughts in his head. However, his mind was made, which meant that he was going to go after Ebony and her henchmen, first, then handle his domestic issues.

It was 10:54AM when he pulled into a diner out in Linkton County where he chose to dine in, hoping to waste a great amount of time. Ordering a large breakfast that he had no intention of finishing; Anthony took his precious time picking at the several dishes for the sake of anybody that could be closely observing him for whatever reason.

About twenty minutes into his meal, Anthony's cellular vibrated atop the table. Seeing the information on the screen, he hurriedly swallowed the portion of pork sausage that he was chewing then took a swig of his orange juice before taking the device in his hand.

"Hello," he answered it.

"Is this Mr. Anthony Hudson?" a masculine voice inquired.

"It is," Anthony replied casting a glance around the restaurant. "Who am I speaking to?"

"I'm Dr. Rubert Shannon," the man announced. "From my understanding, on yesterday, you brought it to my wife's attention that you are at issue with the results of a DNA procedure that I took part in."

"That's correct." Anthony tried to sound formal, though he was suspicious of the man's tone.

"Well, Mr. Hudson," the doctor went on, "in my many years of performing these kinds of procedures, I've never been second-guessed, nor requested to look over any of my analysis."

"I understand."

"However," the man said, "what spiked my interest in your case was the fact that you expressed your theory of the alteration of a document. I was ready to argue anything contradicting my work, but I can never fix my mouth to say anything against falsified documents."

"So, you're a firm believer that your very own documents can be altered?" Anthony posed, now feeling a bit hopeful.

"Any document can be altered," answered Shannon. "In fact, I didn't have to refer to my files to know that the one you left to my wife was not from my office."

"Say what!" Anthony's voice carried across the restaurant.

"Are you anywhere near a fax machine?"

"Not right now," Anthony told him. "If you give me a few minutes I can find one and call you back at this number."

"That's fine. I'll be waiting."

Ringing off, Anthony took one more swig of his orange juice, dropped a twenty-dollar bill onto the table then made for the exit. Upon climbing back into the rental, he accessed the vehicles GPS system to gain the location to a nearby library. Once the location was acquired, Anthony backed out of his spot, and made for his chosen destination thinking about the conversation he had with Dr. Shannon. What exactly did he mean when he said that the document wasn't from his office? It clearly boasted the name of the company that his office is attached to as well as the address. However, as he mentioned, any document can be altered.

Well, Anthony was tired of racking his brains with all of this. When he got to the library, he parked, and rushed inside as if trying to avoid paying late fees for a book he checked out. There was a young brunette at the front desk pulling what appeared to be newly donated books from a box upon her desk.

"Excuse me, ma'am?" Anthony spoke as he approached.

"Yes?" She looked up with agitation written on her face.

"Do you have a public fax machine?"

With only a quick gestation to the left of her, the librarian went back to what she was doing. This didn't bother Anthony because she purveyed him with the information that he needed. Moving to his right, he approached a booth that had three public fax machines. Choosing the one in the middle, he texted the attached phone number to the number Dr. Shannon called him from then waited.

After five minutes had gone by, Anthony was beginning to think that the doctor had been called out on some kind of emergency errand and couldn't entertain him at the moment. Instantly infuriated by the thought, he opened his phone, and was about to call the man back when the middle fax machine beeped, getting his full attention.

Seconds later, there came a whirring sound before a typed document slowly spewed from the machine. The first thing Anthony spotted was the seal belonging to the Linkton County Health Department, which looked the same as it did on the document he turned over to Shannon's wife.

Anxious to see what the inconsistency was between the two documents, Anthony snatched the piece of paper from the machine and took his time scanning it, starting at the company's seal. To him, everything seemed the same. Well, that was until he got to the final part which was the test results that claimed the verdict came out as 99.9.

***

"I don't know, Eb," Samantha was saying to Ebony who was seated across from her in the cafeteria. "That does seem kind of strange. I mean, if I was her, I would've handed the case over to Hendrix, being that he's new and doesn't have much of a caseload.

"Exactly!" Ebony let out sitting her bottled water down too hard causing some to spill onto the table. "You know what? She's conniving and I'm sick of her shit!"

"Well, don't say that too loud!" Samantha cautioned in a hushed tone. "If Barbara ends up like Elizabeth, you'll be Homicides number one suspect.

Ebony bit into her tuna sandwich but said nothing. At that moment, Attorney Ellen Martinez was passing their table carrying her own tray of food. Ebony was intently studying the older woman, so she undoubtedly caught the side-glance that Ellen shot in her direction.

Now, ebony was feeling that there was more to the attorney's apparent fling with her father, which prompted her to think about Bull and Rick. What were they not telling her?

"I know that I really didn't know Elizabeth," Samantha went on. "But I'm still touched by what happened to her. For a man to have strangled her like that, he had to have been in love with her. An ex-lover perhaps."

"You'd make a terrible investigator."

Samantha made a face. "How so?"

"For one, you're automatically assuming that the perp was a man," answered Ebony. "It could have been a woman—a scorned woman."

"That was my next assumption," her friend offered.

Ebony smiled. "Yeah, right."

$$***$$

Upon exiting the library, Anthony got into the rental car and just sat, staring at the copied report he received from Dr. Shannon, while trying to wrap his mind around why Ebony would doctor the results and deprive him of knowing the truth about the man that procreated him. What did she get out of concealing the fact that they were half siblings?

He's been around enough 'daddy's girls' to know how territorial they are about their fathers, but Ebony didn't come off to him as such. Maybe, she was doing this out of spite. Well, whatever her motive, Anthony's mind was already made. Ebony had already sent someone to terminate him, so war had incontestably been declared.

It was approximately 4:49PM when Anthony pulled into the lot of the bakery that sat across the street from the courthouse. After parking where he could see the building, he killed the engine, and began fondling the .380 automatic in his lap. It was sad he wouldn't get the chance to know his father's side of the family, which was something he'd always longed for.

At the thought of this Anthony closed his eyes and shook his head. He was thankful that Ebony had done whatever she'd done to get him out of the situation that he was in, but he was not going to continue living under her thumb and taking orders from her as if he was some kind of flunky, or indentured slave. He definitely wasn't going to live life looking over his shoulder. The only result to that was that one of them had to cease to exist, and Anthony was determined that it was not going to be him.

At twenty-one minutes after five, he spotted Ebony's white Cadillac pulling out of the car garage across the street. It was still daytime but that didn't matter to Anthony. All he wanted to do was catch her at the right moment and finally put all of this nonsense to rest. Pulling out of the bakery's lot, Anthony trailed five cars behind Ebony, until they reached the expressway. That's when he took the far-left lane seeing that she kept to the far right, which was customary, being that her exit was the following one. Aware that his half-sister may have someone following her for security purposes, he made sure to study every vehicle in his immediate vicinity, lest he finds himself caught up in an ambush.

As Ebony's exit was coming up, Anthony eased over into the far-right lane so that he could make the same exit. He found himself four cars behind Ebony when they made it to the off-ramp. At that time, he took to studying the surrounding vehicles again, and kept his head on a swivel as they traveled the main road. After a couple of turns, Anthony spotted some green, older model sedan in his rearview mirror. The first time he laid eyes on the car was on the expressway. Now it was three cars behind him, which meant that the occupant was either part of Ebony's security detail or someone who resides in the same area as her.

Anthony glance at the digital dashboard and noted that they were almost ten minutes out from Ebony's current residence, which wasn't good considering the outlay of the approaching area. There was no way that he would be able to terminate Ebony and overthrow the security detail with ease. Therefore, coming upon the next residential street he turned onto it, figuring he would formulate another plan of action, real soon.

***

Ebony spotted her visitor just before getting on the expressway. The advantage she had over him was the fact that he was an amateur. If he wasn't an amateur, he would have chosen a more inconspicuous vehicle to stalk her in. Clearly, he underestimated the fact that she was a female, and probably thought that she wasn't cautious enough to watch her six.

Not the one to give in to fear, Ebony continued like any other day. Her gun was at the ready, so if he thought that he would be able to catch her off-guard, then he was in for a rude awakening. However, after following her off her exit, he continued his bird-dogging for another moment before turning off on another street. Ebony did not dwell on this being that she had other things on her mind. Of course, it was not going to go unreported. So, upon pulling into her driveway she pulled out her cell phone and dialed Rick's number.

"What's up?" he answered.

"He followed me, today," she let on. "From work."

"So, what happened?"

"Nothing," Ebony told him. "He didn't even follow me all the way home.

"I guess you're ready for us to handle this, huh? Rick surmised.

Ebony sighed. "Not really. I think he's—"

"Why do you keep playing this cat and mouth game with him?" Rick cut her off.

"Excuse me!" she shot back. "I don't know what gave you the indication that I'm playing with him. Let's not forget who's working for who, Rick! Am I taking orders from you now?"

He didn't respond.

"I didn't think so," Ebony continued. "Concentrate on what I pay you to do! In fact, I have a job that needs to be done this weekend. No, make that two."

Chapter 9

"I'm going to adjourn until noon," Judge Jackson promulgated to everyone in the courtroom. "We'll reconvene at about 12:15. That should give everyone enough time to eat something and indulge in whatever it is that you kids like to indulge in, whenever I leave you all unattended."

There were a few snickers about the room as everyone gathered their things and made for the exit. Ebony intended to take her time but Samantha, who was assisting her for the day, was already collecting the documents in front of them and placing then into the accordion folder.

"Let's go, Love Bird!" Samantha said in a hushed tone getting to her feet.

"Say what!" she shot back now standing. Ebony was already infused with crush, so she hasn't been 100% coherent all morning.

"I almost forgot about how you and Judge Jackson always at each other's throats," offered Samantha as they moved towards the exit. "Or should I say *'flirting'* with each other?"

"Your jealous ass would say that" Ebony asserted, fighting the urge to pinch the redhead on her butt when Samantha preceded her through the wooden doors and into the hallways. "You know that I can't stand him."

Samantha smiled. "If that's what you say honey."

"Can I have my briefcase back?"

"When we get to your office," Samantha replied, ringing for an elevator.

Ebony wasn't in the mood to sexually entertain Samantha, but she wasn't going to rain on her friend's fantasy, which would indeed hurt her friend's feelings. She would not hear the last of that. Upon locking her office door, she allowed Samantha to enter first. Samantha placed the briefcase atop the desk before taking a seat in front of it, crossing one leg over the other. This display didn't have the telltale signs of the inception of an impending sexual romp, but Ebony held her peace. Taking a seat behind the desk, she placed her keys and cell phone on top of it, then leaned back in her chair.

"Are we going to spend our recess staring at each other?" Ebony finally asked.

"I want some crush!" Samantha blurted out folding her arms over her chest.

Taken aback by this, Ebony narrowed her eyes at her friend. "Say what?"

"I want some crush," she repeated. "And don't act like you don't know what I'm talking about! I've been around that shit long enough to know how it makes people act. "I also know—"

"Shut up, Sam."

After a few seconds of staring her friend down, Ebony unlocked her bottom drawer, pulled out the pill bottle that contained her personal batch of powered drug, and sat it on top of the desk. The look in Samatha's eyes as she ogled the bottle was akin to that of an ex-drug addict who was about to relapse.

***

Anthony had been out all day mapping out a plan of escape which would avail when he goes after Ebony, again. Considering the mishaps of his first attempt last week, he figured a full plan would have to be devised. Especially being that she was traveling with security detail.

It was close to 8PM when Anthony arrived back at the motel, cautious by nature, while parking the Mazda that he'd traded the Honda in for, he studied every vehicle in the lot just as he studied the window of every room in his view, while headed to his own with a bookbag slung over one shoulder.

Reaching the room, he stopped and turned around, pretending to be searching his pockets for something that he may have left in the car, though he was visibly searching the area, again for anything he may have missed. Satisfied with how everything looked, Anthony finally used the motel key to enter. Just then, at the first sight of the person sitting on the edge of the bed, he reached for the handgun tucked in his waistband.

"That won't be necessary," Ebony offered in he composed tone.

Just as she spoke, Bull stepped out from behind the door and Rick emerged from the bathroom. The first thing Anthony noticed was that they were not visibly carrying. In fact, the only thing that Rick had was in his hand, was a bottled drink. Sitting beside Ebony on the bed, was an iPad electric tablet. With his hand already touching his gun, Anthony felt that he could easily draw his weapon and put an end to the three of them, right then. Of course, he would be wanted for the mass murder but at least he'd be done with this task.

After taking another second to mull over his options, Anthony removed his hand from the gun and closed the door.

"That's more like it," Ebony said, then patted the spot on the bed beside her. "Have a seat my friend!"

Anthony scoffed. "Your friend, huh?"

With no prediction as to how this would end, Anthony decided that he would move with extreme caution around these people, who were just as dangerous as he was. He turned to Bull, who was the closet to him and lifted his sweater. Once Bull lifted the gun off of him, he crossed the room and took a seat beside Ebony placing the bookbag behind them.

"So, we're not friends?" ebony inquired on his reply.

"We're siblings," he told her, casting a glance over at Rick, who was now leaning against the threshold of the bathroom. "Tyrone Davis was my dad also."

Ebony narrowed her eyebrows. "Can you prove that?"

Anthony unzipped the small pouch on his bookbag, pulled the folded document from it, and handed it to her. He waited patiently while she looked over it, though he was anxious to hear what she had to say.

"Where'd you get this?" she finally asked waving the piece of paper.

"From the same place you got yours," answered Anthony. "The original copy—not the one that you had altered and gave to my mom."

"Yeah, whatever!" Balling the piece of paper up, Ebony tossed it onto the floor then looked into his eyes. "Kin or not, I need you to come back."

Anthony didn't respond.

Ebony cleared her throat. "I know that you're on your own road to revenge, so I took the initiative to help you out a bit."

"What do you mean?"

"Kurt is dead."

Anthony was genuinely confused. "And who the hell is Kurt!"

"Janelle's boyfriend," she offered with a smirk. "But you can thank me later."

"I don't believe you," Anthony replied, though he only said it to push her into proving her claim.

"Sure, you do." Ebony lifted the iPad off the bed and began working its functions. "You just want proof."

After a minute of doing whatever she was doing, Ebony handed the device over to Anthony, who found himself watching a YouTube news clip of a homicide that took place in Marrietta, Georgia two nights ago. According to the video clip, Kurtis Manson was gunned down in front of the home that he shared with his girlfriend and he son, upon returning home from work. After showing a picture of him, there was an actual footage of the scene, which was right in front of the house he'd followed Janelle to. Then the clip ended.

"With him out of the way," Ebony resumed taking the iPad from his hands, "You shouldn't have a problem with getting your woman back."

Anthony didn't want Janelle back, but he kept his mouth shut.

"As far as I know," she continued, "Marvin is the last person on your list. Once you're done with him, I need you to come back and honor your contract."

Ebony handed the tablet back to him. On the screen, this time, was a photo of the blonde woman that Anthony had followed on several occasions. The same one he assumed to be Marvin's sister. In this particular picture, he could definitely see their resemblance, whereas they shared the same eyes, nose and mouth.

Anthony looked to Ebony. "Why are you showing me this?" I've already discovered the Marvin has a sister."

A smirk appeared on Ebony's face. "You are so wrong. Marvin does not have a sister."

After regarding Ebony with furrowed eyebrows, Anthony dropped his eyes back to the screen, and instantly felt his blood start to boil. He couldn't believe that he'd gotten that close to Marvin, and the man was still walking around, breathing. He also couldn't believe that Marvin had taken the stolen money and transitioned himself into a woman. Did he do this in order to disguise himself or was he really tapping into his femininity?

Chapter 10

That following morning, Ebony woke up with an extreme headache. It was bad enough that she couldn't reach Samantha last night after leaving Anthony's motel room, which left her going to bed sexually frustrated. Considering that she'd given Samantha drugs earlier, Ebony figured that her friend was probably in a drug-induced coma and had went to bed.

Now upon entering her office, Ebony deposited her briefcase and pocketbook, then took a seat behind her desk. The first thing she noticed was the red indicator on her phone. Figuring it was urgent, she pressed the message button, to see who was anxious to get in touch with her so early. The machine apprised her that she only had one message, followed by a beeping sound, before the highly familiar voice breached the speaker.

"Ms. Davis," Barbara Hutchins started off. "Before you do anything, I need to see you in my office. Don't even report to Judge Jackson's courtroom. This is urgent.!"

Beep!

Ebony leaned back in her chair and ruminated the message. It wasn't the message itself that bothered her, but the tone of the head district attorney's voice. Something was definitely wrong, which had her mind conjuring up a million and one possible scenarios. However, the only one that stuck out was the one where Hutchins lures Ebony into her office where she'd be apprehended by the Fugitive Task Force and charged in the death of Elizabeth Wythe.

Chuckling, Ebony retrieved the pill bottle from her pocketbook and treated her nose before locking the bottle inside the bottom drawer. Then she grabbed her cellular and left the office locking up behind herself.

Still thinking of Samantha, Ebony made sure to stop by the redhead's office only to find the door shut when it's usually open at this time.

"Maybe she hasn't made it in yet," Ebony thought while making for the D.A.'s office.

As always, the door was standing wide open, and Barbara Hutchins was helping herself to a cup of coffee while engrossed in something on her computer screen. Mentally blaming the crush for her actions, Ebony didn't wait for the older woman to grant her entrance. She walked right into the office, and took a seat across from the superior, who now had a disapproving look on her face, which made Ebony smile to herself.

"Are you alright?" Hutchins inquired with a concerned look on her face.

"You said that you wanted to see me," Ebony offered.

"well, of course," said the head district attorney. "Have you had your coffee yet?"

"In your message," Ebony began, "you basically told me to come and see you before I do anything. So, here I am. What's the emergency?"

"It's definitely an emergency," Hutchins avowed, leaning back in he chair. "How are you coming along with that case from Telfair County?"

Ebony shrugged. "I'm still looking at it."

"Well, Scarlatti filed a motion for a speedy trial, and it was granted.

Ebony said nothing.

"The trail starts next week."

"Next week!" Ebony finally came alive. Truth be told, she had not even viewed the first page of the case. "How…"

"Calm down, Ms. Davis!" Barbara Hutchins cut her off, holding a hand up for emphasis. "Today, I'm doing you a favor. I want you to go home, and really familiarize yourself with that case."

"Yes, ma'am!" Ebony got to her feet. "Would that be all?"

"Sure," Hutchins answered. "Go home and put that mind of yours to work! I want you to burn Scarlatti's ass!"

It didn't take long for Ebony to retrieve her things from her office, sign out, and make it back to her car. While enroute to the car garage, she was hoping to run into Samantha but that didn't happen. This was starting to bother Ebony because Samantha was always at work before 8:30a.m, and it was almost nine o'clock. Worried, upon climbing in her car, she started the engine then dialed Samantha's number. When she got the voicemail for the second time, Ebony decided that she was going to drive out to her friend's place.

Ebony hadn't been to Chasity Park in some time, but the rows of mobile homes still looked the same as they did on her last visit. Though her windows were sealed tight, upon pulling through the entrance, she caught a whiff of something burning, but had no idea as to what it was until she drove around the remnants of Samatha's fire damaged trailer and almost fainted.

Slamming the brakes, Ebony pushed the driver's door open and got hung up on her seatbelt while trying to exit. Swearing aloud, she pretty much yanked at the thing. Finally freeing herself, she got out and just stood staring at the large pile of debris that used to be Samantha humble home, which still seemed to be smothering as thin films of smoke arose from it. None of the adjacent trailers were harmed, and it gave Ebony a sense of hope that Samantha's car wasn't present. So, where was the woman in question?

"Did you know her?" The voice came from behind Ebony.

She turned to see and elderly Caucasian woman approaching, clad in a large, gray overcoat, and a brown skullcap that seemed too big for her head though a few strands of silver, curly locks, stuck from under it. Plus, she was using a metal walker to keep her balance.

"Excuse me?"

"Samantha," the older woman said, nodding toward the rubble.

"Did you know her?"

"What happened?" Ebony disregarded the question.

Stopping in front of Ebony, the woman coughed into one of her wrinkled hands before answering. "I think the fire was started around two o'clock this morning. All I know is they woke me up with those loud sirens and fire engines. I knew something was wrong when I smelt the smoke, which smelt nothing like an of the fire barrels that we burn around here."

"When the last time you saw Samantha?" Ebony inquired, thinking about her friends' missing car.

"It was yesterday," said the woman. "I was out with Snooki when Sam returned home from work. She was a prosecutor, you know."

Ebony nodded. "Sure. Do you know if she left back out sometime last night?"

"Samantha didn't hang out," the lady answered with attitude. "Once she's home, that's it. She was a loner, so there was no boy toy to speak of."

"If Sam didn't leave out last night," Ebony posed, "then where's her car?"

"The firemen had it moved out of their way," she told Ebony. "The whole community was up by then. Well, except for the weirdo who stays over there. In fact, I find it strange that he wasn't even home at the time when he barely goes anywhere. Everybody here knows each other, but he's never said one word to anyone since he moved in three weeks ago."

"Are you saying that Sam was inside her trailer when it burned down?"

The older woman looked at Ebony as if seeing her for the first time. "I'm not making this up, young lady. In fact, it's all over the news."

Ebony just stared at her.

"If she was your friend" the woman went on, "I offer my sincere condolence."

***

"Who is it?"

Anthony didn't have to answer the question because the man that he was looking for was regarding him through the transom of the door as though he'd never seen Anthony a day in his life. Well, he couldn't blame the old man because after all, he was a total stranger.

"Hello, sir!" Anthony said, waving a hand, hoping to appear harmless. "Do you remember me?"

The old man furrowed his eyebrows as if he was trying to place the stranger, and wondering if he should open his door to him. Then after a moment of analyzing Anthony, the man began disengaging his security locks before slowly pulling the door open. He was wearing a pair of faded blue jeans and a gray button-down shirt.

"Yeah, I remember you," the man grumbled, looking Anthony up and down. "You were trying to buy that house from Maxine Whyte. How'd that go?"

"We're meeting about it today," Anthony answered looking over at the adjacent house where his rental car was sitting in its driveway.

"Look, sir, I'm only bothering you because I drank too much coffee this morning and it's running through me. May I please use your bathroom?"

As if to see if Anthony's story added up, the man shifted his gaze over to the house next door then back to Anthony.

"Well alright, seeing that we're about to be neighbors and all."

"Thanks, sir!"

Upon the man stepping aside, Anthony entered the home that was quite tidy, but reeked of stale cologne, and some kind of cleaning agents. After locking the door, he motioned for Anthony to follow him.

"Make sure to clean up behind yourself, young man!" the old timer said when he pushed the bathroom door open for him.

"Yes sir!" Anthony replied. "And thanks again!"

Entering the bathroom, and closing the door, Anthony turned on the sink just in case the old fart was standing nearby listening. After counting to twenty, he flushed the toilet, then waited another ten seconds before shutting off the sink water. Unsheathing the hunting knife on his hip, he concealed it up one of his coat's sleeves, then exited.

However, the man was nowhere to be found. Hearing the clinging sound of dishes, Anthony followed his ears, which led him to the kitchen, where the guy was loading the dishwasher. Seeing that his back was turned, Anthony moved as quickly and lightly as possible in his direction.

The man was inserting another load into the washer. Just as he was coming back up, Anthony came up behind him, wrapped on arm around his waist, and jammed the knife into his chest, knowing for sure that it penetrated the guy's heart. Anthony expected some sort of a struggle but didn't receive any. On impact, his body tensed up as he gasped before slowly expelling the last of his breath. Before he could completely expire, Anthony began back peddling, dragging the man's feet as he carried him to the living room where he lay him down on the sofa as if to get some rest. Out of common courtesy, Anthony removed the slippers from the man's feet before lifting his legs onto the sofa. Then he just stood there staring down at the older man, who was staring back up at him, panting softly with both hands rested on his chest, and fingers encircling the blade of the knife that was still protruding from his torso.

At that moment, while watching his victim slowly succumb to his fate, Anthony found himself thinking about his biological father, Tyrone Davis, and wondering if he'd inherited his barbarous behavior from him. As a young boy while watching Tyrome broadcasted trials on television, Anthony was always able to perceive something in Tyrone's eyes that made the hairs on his arms stand up.

However, after experiencing Ebony's cruel demeanor, he knew that the apple didn't fall too far from the tree, which explains why the late Tyrone Davis was so successful as a prosecutor. Of course, Ebony was following in their father's footsteps, and now was destined to make a name for herself.

Anthony was still skeptical about Ebony's request for him to come back to Linkton County, and her taking the initiative to avail him by having Janelle's boyfriend murdered and revealing the current identity of Marvin. He was currently nursing mixed feelings about this because she first sent someone to kill him. Now she wants him to come back and 'honor their contract' as she'd put it.

Surely, she wants him to take over her drug operation because she was on the brink of retiring Rick and Bull, but that could be a rouse to lure him back in, so that she could finish him off herself. He was also struggling with the notion that if Ebony really wanted him dead, she could have easily made that happen on several occasions; especially last night in his hotel room, where he was the epitome of a sitting duck.

Now noticing that the old man had stopped breathing, Anthony withdrew the knife from where it was buried, wiped both sides of its blade on the man's shirt then journeyed off to the main bedroom where he snatched the top blanket off the bed. Returning to the living room, he covered the man with the bedspread, then moved to the window, wondering how long he'd be inside the house with the cadaver before it was time to make his move.

The view from the window was perfect. Anthony could see the house of Louise Atkinson where her SUV was parked in the driveway. Now all he has to do is wait for her peculiar ass son to pay her a visit. Feeling hungry, Anthony made for the kitchen pulling a pair of black gloves from his pants pocket and slipping them on. The first place he checked was the refrigerator, wrinkling his nose at the contents of it. Disregarding the freezer, he slammed the refrigerator's door, and began rummaging through the dry goods cabinets until he came upon some microwaveable popcorn. Placing a bag into the microwave he returned to the living room.

With only a mere glance at the lump lying beneath the now blood-stained blanket, Anthony got to the window and peered out. It was only 12:17PM, so the day was still young. On his initial observation, he concluded that Marvin doesn't visit his mother every single day but didn't go too many days without doing so. His only hope was that Marvin was in the mood to visit the old hag today.

Ding!

Hearing the microwave's bell, Anthony made for the kitchen. After retrieving a bottle of Budweiser from the refrigerator, he grabbed the bag of popcorn and dragged on of the wooden kitchen chairs back into the living placing it at the window. Takin a seat, he twisted the cap off the beer before taking off one of his gloves in order to properly eat his popcorn.

The curtain was left parted, so that he was able to see vehicles passing by the house, though he'd have to stand up in order to actually see the house of Marvin's mother.

Just then, a blue BMW drove by in the direction of Louise's house. There was nothing striking about the care itself, but what really drew his undivided attention was its driver, which was a Caucasian female with blonde hair. Although the car he was looking for was a red Cadillac DTS, Anthony stood to get a better view and saw that the car was entering Louise's driveway, parking behind the SUV. There was no doubt in Anthony's mind as to who the driver was. When his arch enemy climbed from the car and moved towards the house carrying a large paper bag that's when Anthony realized that he was moving on impulse and didn't have a specific plan as to how he was going to handle Marvin.

Scooping another handful of the buttery popcorn into his mouth he watched as Marvin clad in a feminine black trench coat let himself into the house without using a key. That's when a plan started to formulate in his mind. The plan wasn't even one hundred percent established when Anthony slipped his glove back on and moved toward the front door. At this time, the only thing going through Anthony's mind was to not let Marvin slip through his fingers today. It wasn't his intention that Louise winds up harmed in the process, but if she does, then it would be karma for her choosing not to abort the fetus of the son who was now parading around like a freshly baked fruitcake.

Getting into the rental car that was still parked in the driveway of the untenanted house next door, Anthony pulled the .380 handgun that was tucked at the small of his back and tossed it onto the front-passenger seat before climbing behind the wheel. The beer bottle and bag of popcorn were the only items that were capable of placing him at the scene of the old man's murder, which was why he brought them with him. Placing these items wit the gun, he started the car, then backed out of the driveway. Thankful that no one was moving about the neighborhood, he boldly parked at the foot of Louise's driveway and took hold of the handgun. Leaving the engine running, he got out, tucking the gun into the right pocket of his pants where he kept his hand maintaining a grip on it. The taste of revenge became more prominent with every step that he made towards the house. Anthony was so enthralled by the notion of finally putting this all behind him that he was beyond worrying about if he was being watched or not. He only had one mission in mind: Kill Marvin!

Climbing the steps to the porch, Anthony took hold of the handle to the glassed screened door and was surprised at how quietly it opened. He had to release his grip on the gun in order to open the main door, which also came open with ease as he found himself entering the living room. Seeing that no one occupied the room, Anthony listened for any signs of life as he continuously secured both doors one at a time. That's when he realized that the place was eerily quiet. There wasn't even the distant sound of a television playing anywhere. He saw Marvin carry a bag of groceries into the house. Yet, there were no sounds of any groceries being put away or whatnot. After closing the main door, he turned and was about to reach for his gun when Marvin almost seemed to appear out of thin air. He entered the living room from the opposite side, clad in a red turtle-neck sweater, a navy-blue skirt with no shoes on.

On top of moving as swift as military-trained personnel, he was holding some kind of chrome handgun at arm's length with both hands.

Blam! Blam! Blam!

There were three reports from the weapon. Anthony felt two of the slugs slam into his chest and one perforate his right shoulder which sent him into a half spin, causing his head to make contact with the doorknob as he went down, though he remained in a sitting position with his back against the door. There he made a second attempt for his weapon.

"That wouldn't be such a bright thing to do," Marvin advised, moving closer with his gun still aimed.

Marvin's masculine voice was in utter contrast to his appearance. Especially with the long, blonde hair that was pulled into a ponytail, the red lipstick, and the cosmetically engineered breast that pushed against his snug-fitted sweater. Plus, besides being a natural male, his legs were looking quite feminine beyond the black sheer stockings that he was wearing.

"I was wondering when you were gonna show up," Marvin went on. "It's just too bad that things aren't going according to whatever asinine plan you've come up with."

Anthony shot him a confusing look but said nothing as he slowly bled out, and his insides burned from the projectiles that were still lodged inside of him.

"Marvin?" Louise's voice came from somewhere behind her son. "Is it him?"

"It's him, Momma," he answered without looking back. "Go ahead and make the call. Tell them that somebody broke in and I killed him in self-defense."

"He's dead?" Louise sounded frighten.

Marvin bore his blue eyes into Anthony's before answering. "He's very dead."

"Oh, Lord!"

"So, you're gonna kill me, huh?" Anthony inquired when he heard the retracting of Louise steps.

"Had I done that in the first place," Marvin replied, "we wouldn't be in this little predicament that we're currently in. Now, I have to get myself dolled up for the media and prepare to answer a thousand questions. Of course, I'll have to summon a few crocodile tears, which would truly damage a girl's mascara."

Anthony was shaking his head. "I can't believe that you used the money to turn yourself gay."

"A person can't turn themselves gay, Anthony," Marvin told him. "There's no on and off switch to this. You're either gay or you're not."

"You said that you were wondering when I was gonna show up," Anthony reminded, coughing into his left fist. "How'd you know I was out?"

A smile spread across Marvin's face as he lowered the gun to his side. "I assume you pissed the wrong person off," he said.

"Whoever it was, she phoned me two nights ago telling me to watch my back because you were after me and had been watching my mom's residence. Of course, I didn't believe her until I called the Fulton County Jail and was informed of your release."

That's when it dawned on Anthony that Ebony had set him up. His mother knew that he was out, and he was sure that she'd told Janelle but neither of them knew anything about Marvin.

"There sending somebody now, Marvin," Louise informed upon returning.

"Ok Momma," Marvin replied with a glimpse over his shoulder. "I think you should wait in your room."

"Okay."

Anthony already knew that he had 0.00% chance of surviving this ordeal. However, the moment that Marvin looked over his shoulder, Anthony took that chance to make another attempt at his weapon that was still tucked into his pants pocket. Directing his attention back to Anthony, Marvin saw what was taking place but didn't act immediately. It's like he was waiting. Just like a showdown in one of those Western movies, Marvin waited until Anthony had freed his weapon before raising his own.

Pow!

Chapter 11

"Are there any preliminary matters that needs to be addressed before I summon the jury?" asked Judge Jackson.

Ebony was still emotionally dealing with having to witness the burial of her best friend/lover this past weekend, though it was a closed casket procedure. Ebony didn't know any of Samatha's relatives or associates, so she sat at the rear of the church until it was time for her to pay her final respects and chose not to speak to anyone.

Of course, she'd been getting calls from Anthony's mother, Carol, ever since last Thursday, in which she'd been dodging. Carol wasn't a frequent caller, so Ebony was sure that the older woman was only calling to inquire on the death of her son, as if Ebony could fill in the blanks that the news station hadn't.

Anthony wasn't the type to play anyone's rules and Ebony knew this, which was why she felt compelled to set a trap for him. It was incontestable he felt that Ebony was going to have him murdered, hence the reason for the unexpected meeting in his hotel room that night. The pep talk to get him to let his guards down a little.

On the night before the visit, Ebony made contact with Marvin, explained Anthony's intentions and promised to help lure Anthony into a trap. She felt bad about having Janelle's boyfriend executed, but it was all she could think of to gain a small portion of Anthony's trust and it worked out in her favor.

"There's nothing from the State, Your Honor," Ebony now answered the judge's query.

Judge Jackson shifted his gaze to the defense table. "Anything from the defense?"

"Yes, Your Honor," Attorney Rebecca Scarlatti, who was seated with her client, Veron Webb, elegantly rose to her feet. "At this time, the defense is requesting a gag order from the court with respect to the Investigator Ronell Shivers, who will, undoubtedly, testify that he's not the initial investigator in this case."

"So, you don't want Mr. Shivers mentioning anything about being a successor of the initial investigator?"

"Correct, Your Honor."

Jackson raised his eyebrows, "And your reason why this order should be granted?"

"Well, Your Honor," Scarlatti started. "The initial investigator fell ill, which is how Shivers ended up with the case. With him mentioning this, it could make the jury members believe that he's not conclusive to testify about parts of the investigation that he had nothing to do with."

Ebony got to her feet. "Your Honor. The panel of jurors have all been sworn to have fair and impartial minds to all testimonies and evidence."

"That's true, Mrs. Scarlatti," Jackson agreed.

"Your Honor," the defense attorney held her ground. "As far as we know, there's not one person on this panel who's an expert at law. We're putting the defendant's life and liberty into the hands of human beings, who will make decisions based on what's imputed into their natural psyche."

At that moment, it seemed like everything just went still, and everybody in the courtroom were now staring at the attorney. Even an incredulous look for the statement she made. She could just imagine how people around the world were looking at their television, as the preceding was being reported live.

"Is there anything else from the defense?" the judge finally asked.

"Not at the moment, Your Honor," Scarlatti answered before retaking her seat.

He looked to Ebony. "Anything else from the State?"

"The jurors have all been sworn in to have fair and impartial minds to all testimonies and evidence, Your Honor," she repeated, being that was all that she could come up with then took her seat.

Judge Jackson let out an exasperated sigh before addressing the both of them. "Alright after hearing arguments from both parties, I'm going to rule n favor of the defense and grant the gag order. Bailiff, bring in Mr. Shivers!"

Ebony mentally shook her head at the minor defeat as Deputy Aaron Taylor made for the exit of the courtroom. Feeling that all eyes were on her now, Ebony made a show of perusing the documents in front of her.

"I see how this is going already," Corey Briggs, who was assisting Ebony, said in a hushed tone. "If I was a gambling man, I'd put 10 bucks on Scarlatti."

Ebony stopped what she was doing to look into the eyes of the man that she hated more than anyone in the world. He was grinning, revealing those coffee-stained teeth that she wanted so badly to knock down his throat.

"Ten bucks?" she finally spoke. "Is that all you can squeeze out of your little piggy bank?"

His smile brightened, "It sounds like you know a thing or two about four flushing. How about I raise the stakes to one hundred dollars?

"Wow!" Ebony expressed, sarcastically. "That's a whole lot!"

"Okay, Ms. Well-To-Do!" Biggs challenged. "I'll let you call it. What would you like for me to put on the line?"

"Your life," she replied, seriously, staring into his eyes.

Briggs's face instantly became mirthless. In fact, the last time that Ebony looked this serious was when he returned to work from his stress leave, following the kidnapping of his daughter while he was prosecuting Bull's trial.

Though Ebony was still staring Briggs down, she heard the entrance doors opening, which indicated that Taylor had returned with the summoned investigator. Not wanting to leave Briggs in a state of bewilderment throughout the whole preceding, she forced the most plausible smile that she could muster.

"Oh!" Briggs let out with a relieved expression on his face. "Very funny!"

"Yeah," Ebony replied, turning her attention back to the head of the courtroom. "I'm a real hoot."

"Good morning, Mr. Shivers!" Judge Jackson greeted the investigator. "Please take a seat on the stand. We just want to run a judicial matter by you before getting everything underway."

***

It was shortly after five o'clock when Judge Jackson adjourned his courtroom for the day. Being that she had a stop to make before heading home, Ebony rushed back to her office to retrieve her pocketbook, then made her way back to the elevators, hoping to avoid an encounter with Barbara Hutchins, who probably the only someone still present on the prosecutor floor.

Ding!

When the elevator door opened Ebony didn't expect for anyone to be inside but there stood Aaron Taylor in his huge Linkton County Sheriff's overcoat with the fur around its collar and holding the large, round-brimmed hat in his hand.

"Do you mind if I escort you to your car?" he asked, though it seemed like he was mentally bracing himself for a public hanging.

Not wanting to make it seem as if she was expecting this, Ebony lingered a few seconds before saying, "I guess not."

Stepping onto the shaft, she stood beside him placing her back against the rear wall. Of course, Ebony expected Taylor to engage her in conversation, but he was quiet during the whole ride down. Reaching the garage that felt like a large freezer at this time of year, Ebony and Taylor moved in the direction of her car, passing his in the process. After starting her Cadillac by remote, she pulled the driver's door open, then turned to face him feeling that he wanted to say something to her.

"Thank you, Aaron!" she offered, seeing that he was still at a loss for words.

"You're welcome," he responded with a nod. Placing his hat atop his head, Aaron hesitated another moment before diving in. "Look, I apologize for how I've been acting lately. I was just…"

"You don't have to apologize," Ebony cut him off. "I understand. I'm the one who came off a little too strong."

The deputy said nothing.

"I do appreciate the thought, though," she continued, gendering at her watch. "Look I really have to run."

"It's okay," Taylor said, sounding a bit relieved. "Goodnight. I'll see you in the morning."

"Goodnight, Aaron!"

It seemed like Ebony made it to Chasity Park in a matter of minutes. Pulling onto the trailer park's compound, she saw that the remnants of Samantha's home had been cleaned up, but it surprised her that another mobile home had already replaced it, as if Samantha's death was just another of many on God's green earth. The nerve of these people!

Not wanting to drive around the small community as if she was some kind of stalker, Ebony parked in front of the new addition, then exited her car, buttoning the top button of her new coat, and leaned against the driver's door, casually looking around. There were no residents moving about at this time of day, although Ebony was only interested in seeing one person. She had no idea as to which trailer the older woman lived in, or if she was even at home at this time.

Just then she heard the loud creaking sound of a screened door, before seeing a small, short-haired dog, barrel through the door of the trailer on the other side of the dirt road, fervently sniffing the ground, clearly happy to be outdoors. Exiting the home behind the fury animal was the older woman that Ebony encountered on her previous visit to the residence draped in her same gray overcoat and skullcap. Besides the visible look of uncertainty, the woman moved with a purpose as she drew nigh to Ebony in a way one would approach a mentally unstable person.

"Young lady," the woman spoke in a soft tone. "I don't know if you suffer from dementia or any other mental illness, but Samantha is gone. She was inside of that fire."

"I've already accepted that," Ebony responded, ignoring the furtive insult. "Actually, I drive out here to speak with you."

"I'm Trina Norwood," Ebony told her, offering a hand.

"I'm Rose," the woman stammered accepting Ebony's hand, then nodding towards her dog that was still frolicking around. "And that's Snooki."

"Nice dog!" she offered with a smile. "Mrs. Rose, I want to ask about one of your neighbors."

"Samantha, right?"

"No." Ebony gestured with her head. "The guy that lives in that trailer."

Rose gave the indicated mobile home a mere glance before asserting, "There isn't much to say about him. He doesn't associate with anyone here, and he rarely leaves his home."

"It looks like he's not at home right now," Ebony acknowledged.

"In fact, he wasn't home on the morning of the fire. You pointed that out to me, remember?"

"Yeah, I guess I did," Rose admitted with furrowed eyebrows.

"You sound like one of those detectives."

"When's the last time you saw him?" Ebony went on. "Does he even have a name?"

Rose shrugged. "I'm quite sure he has a name, but nobody here knows it. In fact, I haven't seen him since the day before the fire. I mean, he could be out visiting relatives, right?

***

Upon leaving the trailer park Ebony placed a call to Rick telling him to grab Bull and meet her at her place. She didn't expect for them to make it there before her, but she was more than happy to see the black Crown Victoria parked at the curb. They were not occupying the vehicle, but she found them in her living room upon entering the house. Bull was seated in the recliner, and Rick, with his ever-present sunglasses on his face, was seated on the sofa.

"I'm glad you could join us."

"Shut up, Rick!" Ebony scolded, stopping in front of the coffee table and dropping her things onto it. "Right now, I'm moving on a theory, and I have no reservations about it. Once O change into something more recreational, I'll need you two to drive me out to Chasity Park."

"Will we be let in on this theory?" Rick inquired. "Or is this one of those…"

"I'll explain on our way there," she cut him off, retrieved her things from the table, then made for her bedroom.

Ebony already knew what she was looking for, so when she entered her bedroom, it took her no time to find a pair of black jogging pants and sweater, putting them on. While standing at her dresser's mirror combing her hair into a ponytail, she heard someone knocking at the front door, seconds before hearing it open, followed by the sound of an unfamiliar masculine voice.

"Who is that at the door?" she called out but received no response. "Rick? Bull? Who's at the door?"

After another moment of being ignored Ebony let out a sigh and continued with her hair, although she had the feeling that something was amiss. Especially after what happened to Samantha. Finishing up with her hair, she put on her black Official Ladies bubble coat, then topped off her ensemble with a black ballcap while listening out for any kind of sound from the living room. It was still quiet.

"Sen-Tech," she spoke, summoning the home security system.

"I need a visitor count."

"You have zero visitors," the automated voice came from the monitor beside her bed.

"I know damn well…" Ebony mumbled, pulling the handgun from her pocketbook before throwing the strap over her shoulder.

"Sen-Tech, stand by for an emergency distress call. Two minutes."

"Emergency distress call will be activated in zero-two minutes," replied the disembodied system.

With the gun held by her side, Ebony exited the bedroom, cautiously. To her surprise, Bull and Rick were no longer seated in the living room. This was strange because she heard someone knock on the door. She heard other voices but there were no sounds of a scuffle that would indicate that the two men had been harmed. The living room even seemed undisturbed. Not one to have a natural fear for her life, Ebony approached and pulled the front door open, ready to put holes into anyone that didn't resemble her men. However, Bull and Rick were standing on the porch, but they were not alone. The five Solid Nation members seemed to simultaneously drop their gazes to her weapon, then up to her eyes. Though they all appeared a bit alarmed, Rick and Bull weren't fazed by the display.

"Sen-Tech," Ebony shot over her shoulder. "Cancel emergency distress call!"

"Emergency distress call is deactivated," the automated voice came back at her.

"You call up an emergency distress call?" Rick posed.

She leered at him. "Don't question my actions! What's going on out here?"

"Nothing," Rick told her, then regarded the gang. "We'll talk to you boys later,"

Without another word exchanged, the gang member turned, and descended the steps to the porch, while Ebony tucked the gun away inside her pocketbook.

"Do you have everything?" Rick inquired.

"Of course, I do."

There was much attitude in her tone but once again, the older men were unmoved. In fact, they both moved toward the car leaving her to lock the house up. The engine was started, and the heat from the air component had the console warm and toasty by the time Ebony climbed into the back seat of the Ford.

"So, nobody's going to tell me what was taking place on my front porch?" Ebony was determined to not let the uncanny encounter go.

"We're always scouting for new talent," Rick offered, as he pulled away from curb.

"So, you employed those guys without my knowledge?"

"We do a lot of things without your knowledge," he replied.

Ebony shot daggers to the back of his head.

"We got that information for you," Bull offered from the front passenger seat.

Ebony turned to him. "What information?"

"On Tonya Smith," he answered. "The one who Carlos West arrested.

"I'm listening."

"She's a manager at the First National Bank in Linkton County," Bull informed. "She's also married to the owner of the bank, and they have one child."

"I need a home address."

"We got that," he told her. "The next move is on you."

At that moment, Ebony allowed herself to get lost in her thoughts. She knew that it was unethical how she was going about avenging the deaths of her parents, but there was no room in her combatant mind for rational thinking. Had Tonya Smith not filed charges against Carlos West, then Ebony's father would probably still be alive, as would her mother.

"Don't drive inside the compound!" Ebony told Rick once they came upon the Chasity Park community. "Park at the store!"

Doing as he was told, Rick drove further past the locale and pulled into the lot of a small convenience store just next door to the community, making sure to park closer to the street. Before he could kill the engine, Ebony was pushing her door open making her exit.

It was dark out, and the store was closed, which gave Ebony a sense of relief. Plus, there weren't many vehicles travelling along the adjacent road. She stifled a yawn while looking around for anyone that could be out and about but there weren't any.

"Follow me!" Ebony told the men once they'd joined her.

She moved in the direction of the mobile home community but kept past the entrance of it. As they came upon the wooded area that partially obscured the small neighborhood, Ebony did her best to calculate her steps. Once she figured that she'd covered the acquired distance, she turned right and began trekking through the damp earth setting.

"Hold on!" Bull called out from behind her. "There could be snakes out here!"

"Bull, you are entirely too big to be scared of a damn snake!" Ebony shot over her shoulder but kept moving.

Momentarily, they reached the rear of the mobile home that Mrs. Rose had brought to Ebony's attention. Already figuring that the occupant wasn't there, Ebony took it upon herself to peer into the far window, where she knew that the bed would be located, but there wasn't one. In fact, from her vantage point, it appeared that the place was unlived in.

"Come on!" she said, donning her gloves as she moved towards the side of the home.

Although it was dark, the community lamps had the neighborhood highly illuminated, which made it hard for them to proceed unnoticed. However, when they reached the entrance, Ebony pulled the screened door open, turned the knob on the main door, and pushed it open. Just as she figured, the home looked as if it was used as a place of surveillance, considering the various degree of the trash and cigarette butts strewn all over the floor. The strange man had been monitoring Samantha. Ebony didn't have a clue as to who the man was, but she'd wager anything that she knew who his employer is.

"So, what's this all about?" Rick finally asked, pulling Ebony from her abstract musing.

She looked up and realized that she'd taken a seat and was staring out the window at the mobile home that supplanted Samantha's. She also noticed that Bull and Rick were standing over her with their guns drawn.

Ebony looked them both in the eyes before saying, "I know who killed Samantha."

Chapter 12

The following morning, Vernon Webb's trial was back in motion. Rebecca Scarlatti was seated at the defense table with her client and Ebony was standing behind the lectern doing direct examination on a uniform-clad female officer, who was seated on the witness stand.

"So, you were dispatched to the crime scene?" Ebony was asking.

The Caucasian woman nodded her head once. "Yes, I was."

"First to arrive?"

"The very first," she answered.

Ebony shifted her weight. "And what was your initial discovery?"

"Upon arriving on the scene," she answered, "my partner and I discovered the body of 11-year-old Malcolm Tinsley, who was missing approximately 23 days at that time."

"What was the condition of the subject?" Ebony wanted to know.

Scarlatti lunged to her feet. "Objection, Your Honor!"

"Under what grounds?" Judge Jackson inquired.

"The prosecutor is endeavoring to coerce this witness into answering a question that she's not at liberty to answer."

"Your Honor," Ebony stood her ground. "The witness has already admitted to finding the body of the 11-year-old missing child. I don't see any reason why..."

"Only the crime scene investigator should be allowed to answer anything pertaining to the condition of the crime scene in this delicate case, Your Honor," Scarlatti cut her off.

"That's true, Ms. Davis," the judge sided. "The witness did admit to finding the subject. However, it rests upon the crime scene technician to present such evidence to the court. With that being said, I'm going to sustain objection. State, you may continue."

Ebony had already expected this. Though she had a legitimate rebuttal to the attorney's objection, she knew that Scarlatti would succeed, considering the influence she has over judges; but Ebony refused to let one minor set-back throw her off her game.

"Officer Poole," Ebony resumed. "How were you able to identify the subject as Malcom Tinsley?"

"I watch the news." The officer replied with a hint of an attitude. "Plus, after the Amber Alert was put out, computer generated photos of him were put up all over the police stations and inside our squad cars."

"So, you've pretty much committed his features to your memory bank, right?"

The woman nodded. "Yes."

"What did you do after recognizing the lost child?" Ebony ventured. "Were you able to get some kind of response from him?"

Officer Poole regarded Ebony with a look of uncertainty.

"Malcolm was already deceased when we arrived on the scene."

Ebony didn't know why, but she lingered for a bit to allow for the officer's words to sink into the minds of everyone in the court room, or perhaps, she was bidding herself time to calculate her next move.

"Nothing further, Your Honor," she finally spoke, moving towards her table, where Corey Briggs was seated with a smug look on his face.

Judge Jackson looked to Scarlatti. "Cross?"

"No, Your Honor," the attorney answered.

"May this witness be released?"

"Yes, Your Honor," Ebony and Rebecca replied in unison.

"Officer, you are released," Jackson announced, nodding for Deputy Taylor to escort her out. "At this time, I'm going to call a recess. I want everyone to back here in one hour."

Ebony was glad that the judge had called a recess because she was famished as a result of not eating anything earlier. For breakfast, she only helped herself to a hefty dosage of crush and a cup of coffee.

Since the passing of Samantha, trips to the cafeteria has been solo ventures for Ebony which was why it came as a surprise when Aaron Taylor offered to treat her to lunch. Figuring he had something to talk to her about and more than anxious to hear him out, she took him up on his offer, which was why they were seated across from each other in the cafeteria.

"I do miss her," Ebony was saying before taking a sip of her bottled water.

"Yeah, I know," he replied, jostling the contents of his salad around with his plastic fork.

He seemed to be lingering.

"Is there something you want to talk to me about Aaron?" Ebony prompted.

"I, umm…" the deputy stammered. "I apologize for how I've been acting towards you."

"We've already been through this," she told him. "How many times are you gonna apologize for that? There's something else on your mind. What is it?"

Aaron let out a sigh before saying. "Kendra is filing for a divorce."

"I'm sorry to hear that!" Ebony lied, as she spotted Attorney Ellen Martinez entering the cafeteria carrying an older model briefcase that stood out her in the mind of the one that was delivered to her grandparents' home, succeeding the deaths of her parents.

"That's life," he offered with a shrug. "I mean, nothing lasts forever, right?"

"Pretty much."

***

"I'm not trying to be at this all night," Ebony said from the rear seat of the SUV that was driven by Bull. "I do have trial in the morning."

"We already know this," Rick now replied from the front passenger seat. "How long we stay inside is totally up to you."

Ebony wanted to give him a piece of her mind, but he was actually right. She was the boss. She called all the shots. When she says *'go'*, they go. When she asks questions, they answer, which reminded her of what she wanted to talk to Rick about.

"Rick, I need to ask you something," she finally spoke.

"Okay," was all he replied with.

"You delivered a briefcase full of money to my grandparents' home after my parents died," Ebony dived right in noticing the look that Bull shot across to him. "Was the money already inside the briefcase when you found it at the house of Wilks, or did you put it there?"

"It was already there."

"For an upcoming drug deal?"

"There wasn't any upcoming drug deal at that time," Bull answered. "That had to be a payout."

"A payout for what?" inquired Ebony, though she already knew the answer.

Bull shrugged his shoulders. "For a job, I guess."

"I don't know why," Rick chimed in. "But your dad always used briefcases for those kinds of jobs."

"So, who was the job?" she asked, quickly catching on. "I mean, if the money was still there that means the job was never done, or the person never paid. Which is it?"

Neither one of the men cared to answer. This made Ebony angry because she felt that the two of them were withholding information pertaining to the last moments of her parents' existence. Considering this, she drew the handgun from her clutch bag and cock the chamber.

"We're not doing this shit!" Ebony voiced. "You two promised me closure on the death of my mom and haven't offered me one piece of information pertaining to her. Well, tonight's the night. And don't everybody speak at one time!"

Still the men refused to respond. She thought they would at least exchange a glance but didn't even bat an eye at her demand. With more fire added to the flame, Ebony aimed the gun barrel at the stereo system.

Pow!

"What the fuck!" Bull let out as he fought to gain control of the truck after reflexively swerving into the opposite lane.

"Was that even necessary?" asked Rick, who hadn't flinched at all.

Ebony was too upset to answer.

"Your parents were getting a divorce," Rick went on.

"I already knew that," she spat. "Tell me something I didn't know!"

"Did you know the reason?"

Ebony shrugged. "Of course. My mom got tired of him cheating on her."

"Your mom was no Virgin Mary herself."

"Excuse me!" Ebony flared up.

"Your dad found out that your mom was having an affair with a white man by the name of John Carpenter," Rick pointed out. "John Carpenter had HIV and passed it on to your mom. She passed it on to your dad."

"Say what!" Ebony was determined to not allow herself to believe such nonsense. "Why should I be…"

"Get their autopsy reports," Rick cut her off. "Even Carpenter's."

Ebony knew better to wrangle any further because the older man had a valid point. For him to make such a suggestion, it meant that his assertion probably reigned true. Knowing that there were other things she wanted to know, she decided to change her line of questioning.

"Tell me about Ellen Martinez," Ebony resumed. "The lawyer."

Rick asked, "What about her?"

"How close were she and my father?"

"They were close enough."

Ebony furrowed her eyebrows. "That's not telling me anything. Has she ever done a job for him?"

"Of course, Rick answered. "She was on the Sara Jennings job and a few others. In fact, he called upon her for a job just before he died.

"What kind of job?" Ebony inquired thinking about all the furtive ways the Latina attorney regard her.

"I don't know," the older man gave with a shrug. "I can't even say if the job ever got done, being that the payment was never delivered.

"That would be the briefcase, right?"

Rick nodded his head up and down.

"That's the house right there!" Bull apprised docking the truck in front of the house that sat across from the one he indicated.

Though the wheels in her head were turning something furious, Ebony still managed to force herself to direct her attention across the street. The red-brick home had a gray, mid-sized Mercedes truck and a black Chrysler van sitting in its driveway. It was only minutes before eight o'clock, so it seemed that every light inside the house were on, which indicated that the occupants were well awake.

Rick nodded back at Ebony. "It's your call," he told her.

"I want you to pick the locks," she replied, with her mind back on business. "We should be in and out within ten minutes give or take."

"What about masks?" Bull wanted to know.

"We won't need any," Ebony told him.

Knowing that it was his move, Rick climbed down from the truck and looked both ways while crossing over to the targeted home. They watched as he approached the front door. They couldn't see what he was doing when he reached it, but they knew he was breaching the security locks, which took no time. When Rick gave the signal that everything was done, Bull killed the engine as Ebony donned her gloves. Upon exiting the SUV, she pulled the bib on her cap lower and crossed the street with Bull at her heels, though Bull proceeded her by the time they reached the steps of the porch.

Seeing the inquisitive look that Rick was giving her, Ebony nodded in response. That's when the two men brand sided their pistols before Rick pushed the front door open leading the way inside. The first room was the living room where a teenage boy who looked to be thirteen years of age was lying across a sofa watching television. Upon their entrance, he began to slowly move into a sitting position, though he didn't seem at all alarmed.

"You can sit up," Ebony told him pulling her gun from her bag as Rick and Bull exited the room to search other parts of the house. "But I advise you not to leave that sofa."

The kid only nodded as his eyes remained transfixed on the weapon that wasn't aimed at him. Moments later, Rick re-entered the room behind Bobby Stevens, who had his fingers interlocked behind his head, and fear registering in his blue eyes. Quickly sizing up the scene, he obediently sat at the other end of the sofa, opposite his son, who clearly shared his prominent facial features.

Just as his behind made contact with the cushion, Tonya Smith-Stevens was ushered in by Bull. The woman who's responsible for the boy's dark hue and touch texture of hair, entered hesitantly, wringing her hands in front of her protruding belly that was a result of being about six months into her pregnancy. Her frantic eyes instantly took in the whole scene but when they landed on Ebony, there was a sign of recognition registering in them. If Ebony was reading it right, it seemed like the consternation had redoubled within her pupils.

"I assume that you know who I am?" Ebony spoke once the gravid woman had placed herself between her son and husband.

Tony dropped her head in response.

"I'll take that as a yes," Ebony resumed. "So, you probably know why I'm here."

"I understand why you're here," Tonya admitted, now raising her eyes to meet Ebony's. "I just don't see the logic in it. I mean, neither one of us had anything to do with your father's death."

"Oh?" Ebony expressed, looking as if she'd been struck. "If I can recall correctly, a certain individual had another individual arrested for assault because she couldn't control her sexual desires. Had you not gotten caught with your mouth full, Carlos West would have never went to jail, and my father would probably still be alive."

"I didn't call the police," Tonya tried to reason. "My neighbors heard the commotion, and…"

"What's your name kid?" Ebony asked the boy, clearly disregarding Tonya's explanation.

The teenager looked to his parents as if for permission.

Ebony stepped closer to the coffee table and aimed the gun at him. "I'm talking to you!" she raised her voice. "What is your name?"

"D-Darren," he stammered.

"Tonya Smith?" Ebony spoke though she maintained eye contact with the child. "Do you take full responsibility for my father's death? And I advised you to be extremely careful of how you answer that question.

Tonya shot a frantic look to her son then back at Ebony. "I, um…"

Pow!

The report caused both husband and wife to flinch out of fear, but the sole slug penetrated Darren's left breast plate. His eyes widened from the shock before looking down at his wound, but he never looked back up. When her son quickly succumbed to his wound, a grieving Tonya took hold of his drooping head and laid it in her lap. Rick crossed over to the window and peered out, which was a reminder to Ebony that they probably didn't have long before the authorities arrived, following a call from one of the neighbors. Ebony turned her gun on Bobby.

"You don't listen too well Tonya," she taunted, regarding the woman through narrowed slits. "You can't answer one simple question, truthfully. Why can't you just take responsibility for your actions?"

Tonya raised her teary and hate filled eyes to meet Ebony's

"I'm going to ask you one more time," Ebony resumed ignoring the look. "Do you, Tonya Smith-Stevens, take full responsibility for my father's death?"

"Yes," Tonya said, forcefully. "I do."

"Thank you!"

In one swift gesture, Ebony turned the gun from Bobby to Tonya, and squeezed on the trigger. The woman's left eye socket exploded on contact as she died instantly, slumped over her expired offspring. With that, Ebony stuffed the gun back into her bag then spun on her heels.

"Somebody, grab those shells!" Ebony ordered as she made for the door.

"What about him? Bull inquired.

With one gloved hand poised on the doorknob, Ebony looked back and replied: "Is he competent enough to stand trial?"

Without awaiting an answer, Ebony let herself out, aware of what was about to take place. The shot rang out just as she cleared the bottom step. Mentally checking Tonya Smith off her list, she made for the SUV, wondering how she was going to handle Governor Albert Spires.

Chapter 13

Winters cleared his throat. "Well, a copy of the entire report is forwarded to the investigating official, along with the property of the subject, and any loose evidence. In this case, the loose evidence was the plastic cord affixed the victim's neck. One copy is filed into my personal files, another goes into our digital archive."

"Does the chief examiner sign off on these reports?"

"Of course," Winters replied as if answering an asinine question. "That's what solidifies the final ruling."

"So, there would be three signatures?" Scarlatti continued, seeming unfazed. "Yours, the senior's, and the chief's, correct?"

"That's correct."

"Did you sign this particular report?"

"Yes, I did."

"Did the senior examiner sign?"

"Yes."

"What about the chief examiner?"

"The chief examiner signed also."

Scarlatti raised an eyebrow. "Are you sure about that?"

"All reports have to be signed by the chief," Winters voiced not bothering to conceal his agitation.

"Are you sure that the chief signed this particular report?" the attorney further taunted.

The M.E. glared at her.

"Objection, Your Honor!" Ebony decided to intervene from her seat.

"Grounds?" Judge Jackson asked.

"She's badgering the witness," Ebony offered.

Scarlatti turned to the judge. "Your Honor, the question is to get further confirmation and doesn't fit the definition of *'badgering'* in any state, nation, or country."

Jackson rolled his eyes. "Objection overruled. Mr. Winters, please answer the question!"

"Yes, the chief examiner signed that particular report," the examiner answered obediently.

"Thank you, Mr. Winters!" Scarlatti said sweetly before turning back to the judge. "Your Honor, may I approach the witness?"

"Any objection from the State?" he asked.

Ebony shook her head. "No, Your Honor."

"You may approach counsel."

"Thank you, Your Honor!' Rebecca Scarlatti took hold of the file and placed it down in front of the medical examiner before re-taking her place behind the lectern. "Now, Mr. Winters, what I just placed before you is what's been marked as State's Exhibit Four. Could you tell the court what this is?"

After a mere glance at the folder that was opened in front of him, he replied: "My analysis report in this case.

"If you will," she continued. "I want you to take a few seconds to look over the contents of that file."

Winters took a moment to sift through his work. When he was done, he looked up at the attorney.

"Are you ready?" she asked.

He nodded. "Yes, I am."

"Now, we've already established that there would be three signatures of confirmation following the conclusion of your analysis," Scarlatti let on. "That would be yours, the senior, and that of the chief examiner. Right now, Mr. Winters, I want you to choose any one of those documents, and point out the signatures belonging to yourself, the senior examiner, and the chief examiner, if you will."

Again, the attorney thrusted a hand upon her hip and watched as the medical examiner attentively searched through the files. Seeing the turbid look on the man's face made Ebony wonder what Scarlatti could be up to. For her to deliberately target the validations of the medical personnel's signatures, this meant that she was on to something, like a hound dog on the trail of a wounded animal.

Ebony only skimmed through the file, so she really couldn't fathom the attorney's method in order to conjure a way to combat it. Switching her gaze, she saw the amused look etched on Scarlatti's face, which showed that she was enjoying this little sideshow of hers that could very well be a vital loophole in the case.

Finally, Mr. Winters looked up from the file. "I see what you're getting at."

"Excuse me, Mr. Winters?" Scarlatti pose with that amused look still lingering.

"There's only two signatures," he offered, slowly shaking his head. "I forgot that the chief examiner was out on sick leave."

Although the signature mishap wasn't some kind of dirty, underhanded scheme perpetrated by the attorney, Ebony came to the conclusion that she was done with playing fair. Scarlatti had humiliated her once, and Ebony was highly determined that it wouldn't happen again, which is why she placed a call to Rick just upon leaving the courthouse.

"I think I can make that happen," the older man's voice now filtered through the phone.

"I don't need you to think, Rick," Ebony hissed as she switched lanes on the expressway. "I need you to make it happen. This is very important to me."

"You've already made that clear, Ebony," he shot back. "I'm quite sure that I can made that clear Ebony," he shot back. "I'm quite sure that I can make it happen. I just have to figure out who I'm gonna make it happen with. But you'll have to give me a minute."

"I don't have a minute."

Glancing up into her rear-view mirror, Ebony spotted the green Cadillac that was four car links behind her. She'd told Rick and Bull about the suspicious vehicle, but not in the sense to alarm them. However, now as she eyed the car, she thought about what her father said about somebody she'd sent to prison coming back to blow her brains out, which is practically what happened to him. This sent chills up her spine.

"Well, better find one!" Rick shot back pulling Ebony from her abstract musing. "Or find someone else to do the job."

She was taken aback by the response. "Rick how dare you sp…"

"Call disconnected," the car's disembodied Bluetooth system informed.

"No shit!" Ebony retorted, looking up in the rear-view mirror.

The Cadillac was still four cars directly behind her. Although she was experiencing a twinge of fear, she made an instant decision not to become a prisoner to such emotions. At that moment, Ebony initiated her right-turn signal the eased into the adjacent lane. It was still daylight so while keeping an eye on the Cadillac through her mirror, Ebony could tell that its occupants was wearing some kind of ballcap. She was certain it was a male. However, she couldn't decipher if he was Caucasian, or a light complexion black man.

"Let's see if I can identify you."

Ebony eased her foot off the gas pedal allowing her car's speed to decelerate hoping that the move seemed innocent in the eyes of her stalker, or whatever he considered himself as. The car that was originally behind her passed the driver's side of her car subsequently followed by the second one. Before the third car roared by, Ebony noticed that the older Cadillac also seemed to be dropping back. The honk of a horn caused her to look up in her rear-view mirror at a dark colored brown van behind her that was a little too close to her bumper. To avoid impact, she pressed down on the gas pedal to regain speed. Just as she did, Ebony saw the Cadillac slide in behind the van, indicating that the occupant was on to her. Remembering the gun in her purse on the seat beside her, she retrieved the weapon and placed it in her lap.

"I'm not going out like Samantha," Ebony mumbled keeping her eyes on the mirror. "At least not today."

Chapter 14

Atlanta, Georgia
Saturday

"Would you come on woman!" Albert Spires called out as he took another look at his watch.

The NAACP Accreditation Luncheon was being held today. Sure, there were one hundred and one other things that he'd rather be doing, but he was set to present an honorary badge to a long-term organizer of the NAACP in the Atlanta region. To decline would give his reputable image a black eye, which would not look good on him. Especially with the elections just around the corner.

Now, after tying, and adjusting his necktie in the large mirror mounted on the closet's door, the governor of Georgia crossed over the bed, where Lilly, the youngest of the housekeepers, was rolling a barbaric roller over his charcoal-colored blazer that was lying across it. Seeing the way her skirt sunk between her buttocks, pushed the start buttons on his hormones. After taking a gander at the bathroom's door to make sure that Jennifer wasn't coming out of it, he lifted the skirt a bit and let his pudgy hand make its way to her close shaved vagina, in which the redhead gave no kind of response to. As always, Lilly wasn't wearing any panties, so his fingers were instantly met by the warm liquid that stood sentry at the entrance of her love mound. Just then, finished with what she was doing, the housekeeper stood erect, drilling her green eyes into his.

"You really need to consider what I told you," he said, in a low tone to the woman that always reminded him of the late Samantha Gordon, who was dead because he'd given the green light to end her existence. "You know I don't need this shit on my name."

"Why'd you say that, Albert?" she hissed. "You act like your disgusted by the fact that I'm having your child, but it wasn't disgusting for you to have unprotected sex with me."

"Watch your tone, Lilly!" Albert threatened looking over his shoulder at the closed bathroom door. "It's for the best. You're gonna have the abortion, or else!"

"Or else what, Albert?" the young woman challenged with arched eyebrows. "Are you gonna have someone murder me?"

He scowled at the housekeeper.

"Is everything alright?" Jennifer's voice came from behind him.

Albert turned to face her, holding his arms out for Lilly to help him into his blazer. "Everything is fine, sweetheart. Are you about ready?"

"Mm-hmm."

While the housekeeper assisted the governor with his coat, Jennifer, who was clad in a platinum Angel Cofer evening gown, and matching pumps, crossed over the dresser, and began applying her favorite lip balm. She couldn't make out what was said between the two of them while she was in the bathroom, but she was highly aware of what he had going on behind her back. Plus, she could tell by the growth in the young woman's stomach that she was a little over two months pregnant.

Lilly's not the first, nor only housekeeper that Albert had had his way with, in his little secret room that he thought Jennifer had no knowledge of. However, she was sure that her husband was unaware of the affair that she was having with Sanchez, Albert's head of security.

Knock! Knock! Knock!

"Are you guys ready?" asked Sanchez, who was now standing in the threshold of the open bedroom door.

"Give us five more minutes, Sanchez!" Albert told him, "Yes sir!"

Seconds after Sanchez disappeared, Lilly made her exit, leaving the couple to do last minute preparations, which were in complete silence. Moments later, Albert and Jennifer were met at the entry hall by Sanchez and two other members of the security detail.

The muffled sound of machinery run by the landscaping detail out, out front, became intensified when one of the men opened the front door for them to exit. In the large driveway, sat the governor's stretched Cadillac, which was accompanied by two other cars, where three other security personnels stood around.

As they traversed toward the convoy, Jennifer attention was on the members of the landscaping detail. Neither of them looked familiar, being that they were African American, and the original crew were all Hispanic. Something wasn't right.

"Sanchez?" Jennifer turned to the large man. "Where's the original crew?"

He shrugged his shoulders. "I have no idea. Lopez never called in. These guys showed up, and immediately went to work."

Hearing this caused Albert to look in the direction of the detail who were all black. The van and super cab pick-up truck sported the same company's logo that Lopez was sub-contracted to. Plus, these guys were wearing white caps, gloves, and jumpsuits, which was unusual. Another thing he found unusual was how they were all standing at proximity. Two men were sitting on idling mowers that were facing one another; two were operating weed eaters practically side by side; one was operating a leaf blower in front of the van, while another operated one closer to the trailer hitched onto the truck that sat behind the van. There were also men seated behind the wheel of each vehicle with one man looking as though he was rummaging around the rear compartment of the van.

Albert's eyes were still on the crew as he and his detail neared the cars. Just then the man at the rear of the van stepped back brandishing an assault rifle. The other men seemed to draw weapons out of thin air, but Albert's focus was on the figure that emerged from the rear of the van. Though this person was dressed in the same manner as the others, he could tell that it was a female by the gait, body form, and the fine hair pouring from underneath the cap. As the woman's features became recognizable, Albert immediately began to regret his decision on postponing her fate. Sanchez and his men were unaware of what was transpiring until the first round of shots rang out, as the faux landscape workers slowly converged on them. The guards couldn't get their weapons out quick enough. Albert could see their bodies dropping to the ground from his periphery as he kept his eyes on the woman who was approaching in a menacing stride, with a silver handgun down at her side. Even Jennifer was gunned down in the ordeal. Seeing that he hadn't been hit yet, and he was close to the stretch Cadillac, Albert yanked the rear door open, threw his bulk onto the seat and pulled the door shut, pressing down on the lock button. By this time, the gunfire had ceased, and Albert knew that he was the only one still living, though he didn't know for how long.

Reaching the door, Ebony rapped on the thick window with one of her gloved hands, then glowered at him. When she turned and moved toward the front of the car that's when Albert realized that the doors up front were possibly unlocked.

Click!

First, he heard the front door opening. Then, he felt the light dip of the car's suspension when Ebony Davis sat down in the front passenger seat. As the partition window began to roll down, Albert looked out the side window at the eight, dangerously armed men and figured he'd take his chance with his sole arch enemy up front.

"You don't listen too well, fat boy!" Ebony sneered as she was turned in her seat with the gun hanging over the threshold of the divider. "I told you to leave Samantha out of it, but you refused to obey. I also told you that I am a very powerful woman, and you chose to call my bluff. Now, look at you! I just wiped out your whole security team in less than a minute, and you're sitting back there looking like a scared orphan. Now, how's that for a stray monkey?"

"Surely that didn't hurt your feelings," Albert Spires offered in a composed tone. "I'm quite sure you've been called way worse."

Ebony didn't reply.

"Look, Mrs. Davis," he tried using the formality card. "Why don't you accept my apology, and we try and work something out?"

"We did work something out," Ebony replied. "I told you that if anything happened to Samantha, I would flip that mansion overlooking for you, and that I was taking no prisoners. You did your part, now it's time I do mine. Make sure to tell Sam that I'll always love her."

Albert opened his mouth to say something, but Ebony's finger was already pulling the trigger back, sending a barrage of bullets at the rotund governor. Even after the cartridge ran dry, she squeezed the trigger a few more ties before letting the gun fall from her hand.

***

It was still daytime when Rick pulled the van around to the back of the industrial building, making sure to park further away from the unmarked Ford and the GMC Yukon belonging to the six, Solid Nation members, who were now trailing them in the super cab pick-up. When Rick brought the van to a halt, the pick-up stopped directly behind them. At that time, Bull, who was stationed in seatless cargo area, handed Rick a nickel-plated AR-15, then checked the cartridge of his own AK-47. Ebony looked over at her henchmen.

"I'm exhausted," she told them. "Make this quick!"

Without a word, Bull moved to the rear door of the van. As he pushed the doors open, Rick was stepping out and moving toward the pick-up like a trained soldier. Ebony couldn't tell whose weapon went off first and she didn't care. She was just ready to get home so that she could get high and soak in the tun for a few hours.

While her men were executing the Solid Nation group, Ebony got out and began peeling off the white jumpsuit that was already uncomfortable. By the time that she was able to get one leg out, the gunfire had ceased.

After tossing their weapons into the van, Rick and Bull also started shedding their suits. The hat and rubber gloves were the last items that Ebony tossed inside the van before heading for the Ford, without as much a mere glance in the direction of the bullet riddled truck with its deceased occupants.

"Rick, I don't know why you're being so naïve," Bull spoke after peering around the van to see that Ebony was out of ear shot. "Once she's done with us, we'll be just like these guys."

Tossing his jumpsuit inside the van, Rick took a look back at the dead men in the truck before saying, "She gave us her word."

Rick didn't answer. A part of him felt that his friend was right, but another part of him wanted to believe Ebony, who's occasionally showed great interest in him. Surely, she wouldn't go back on her word right?

"The apple doesn't fall too far from the tree, Rick," Bull tried again, tossing his own jumpsuit into the van. "We need to get her before she gets us. In fact, there's no better time than now. Nobody knows she's here. We can knock her off and go on with our lives. We're too old for this shit man!"

"I can't believe you're talking like that!" Rick hissed.

"What!" Bull appeared hurt.

"If it wasn't for her," he went on, "your ass would be sitting on death row right now, waiting to be executed."

"Hell, what's the difference?" Bull shot back. "I still feel I'm waiting to be executed. At least on death row they give you a date, and let you talk to some boot-legged ass pastor before frying your ass."

Rick regarded his friend for a moment before grabbing one of the gasoline cans and handing it to him.

"Fry the damn van so we can get the fuck up out of here!"

Retrieving the other can, Rick cast a glance over at Ebony, who was leaned against the Crown Victoria with her arms folded over her chest and he head down as if in deep thought. The widows were down on the pick-up, so as he doused the cadavers in the flammable liquid, Rick was wondering what she could possibly be thinking about.

Whoosh!

The sound of the van going up in flames pulled Rick from his thoughts. This let him know that it was time to go. Tossing the empty gasoline can inside the truck, Rick stepped back to let Bull toss the already sparked flare through the driver's window. The second that the console ignited, Rick spun on his heels and moved towards the Ford with Bull trailing behind.

Rick disarmed the alarm with the key fob and Ebony immediately climbed into the front passenger seat. Once he and Bull joined her, Rick started the car then drove around the warehouse building headed for the main road. When they entered onto the road, Rick turned the radio on, which only won him a disapproving look from Ebony before she took it upon herself to turn it off.

"What's the word on the woman?" she asked.

"I'm still working on her," Rick replied.

Ebony turned to him. "I need her ready by Tuesday Rick!"

"I'll do my best," Rick gave in as he brought the car to a stop at a traffic light.

Stifling a yawn, Rick looked back at Bull, who was seated behind Ebony, to see that Bull was staring back at him. The look on his face was unreadable, but Rick's focus was on the handgun that his friend was fingering in his lap. Thinking nothing of it, he looked back out of the front windshield to see if the stoplight had changed.

Pow!

Rick didn't have to look back to see what just transpired, but he did. It was almost like he could see the smoke rising from Bull's gun. Plus, Bull was regarding him with that same unreadable look. Ebony was also looking at him, but her expression was part frightened and part shocked, ad blood spilled from her mouth. There was also blood seeping through her shirt between her breasts, indicating that Bull had shot her through the seat. Despite the look that she was giving him, she was holding her palms up as if asking him how could he let Bull do that to her.

"Rick?" she called his name calmly as if she was confident that he could fix everything at that moment.

In response, Rick looked back at Bull, who was now smiling at him, almost tauntingly. Loyal to a fault, Rick found himself stuck between a rock and hard place because he was loyal to the both of them, and he knew that he couldn't take one's side over the other.

"Rick?" Ebony called out to him again.

Snapping out of his abstract musing, Rick looked over to Ebony to see that the blood was all gone as if it had never been there. Bull's gun was sitting in his lap, and he was no longer smiling, but regarding Rick with a concern expression, similar to the one on Ebony's face.

"The light's green," she told him, gesturing with her hand.

"Yeah," was all Rick could say before moving the car along.

Chapter 15

Monday

"State, your witness," Judge Jackson said after Detective Ronell Shivers was sworn in.

Getting to her feet, Ebony rounded the State's table with a manilla folder in her hand and emplaced herself behind the podium. After placing the folder down in front of her, she opened it up and pretended to study a couple of pages before regarding the homicide detective.

"Good morning, Mr. Shivers!" Ebony finally spoke. "I am Ebony Davis, the prosecutor in this case, and I'm going to ask you questions pertaining to your involvement in this investigation."

"Okay," Shivers replied with a nod.

Ebony looked to the judge. "Your Honor, may I approach the witness?"

"You may," he responded.

Scooping the file up, Ebony placed it down in front of the detective, then returned to the podium.

"Mr. Shivers," she began. "I just placed a file in front of you. Could you take a second to look that over?"

He did, then looked back up at her.

"Can you tell the court what that is, Mr. Shivers?"

"It's my investigative report of the Malcom Tinsley case," he answered.

"Is it the full report?" inquired Ebony.

"Yes, ma'am."

She turned to the judge. "Your Honor, the State would like to enter this file into evidence."

"Any objections from the defense?" he asked.

Scarlatti replied, "No, Your Honor."

Judge Jackson nodded to Ebony. "Evidence is admitted."

"Thank you, Your Honor!" Ebony took the file over to Briggs, who stamped it.

When he handed it back to her, she retook her place behind the lectern, opening the folder up in front of her.

"Mr. Shivers could you again tell the court how you are employed?"

"Yes," he answered, clearing his throat. "I'm a Tattnall County Homicide Investigator."

"On March seventh of two thousand and twenty-three," she went on, "were you called to investigate a homicide?"

The investigator shot her a skeptical look before regarding the judge with the same expression.

"Objection, Your Honor!" Scarlatti was on her feet.

"Grounds?" asked Jackson.

"Misleading the witness," she said with attitude.

"Sustained." He looked to Ebony. "State, please rephrase your question."

Ebony exhaled before asking, "Mr. Shivers on what date did this investigation start?"

"It was on the 7th of March," he answered. "Two thousand and twenty-three."

"And what were your discoveries on this date?"

"The body of Malcom Tinsley was discovered," replied Shivers. "Plus, several items of evidence

Ebony raised an eyebrow. "Such as?"

"Particles of clothing belonging to the deceased 11-year-old," he answered. "If I'm not mistaken, there was a bookbag with school supplies in it, and a damaged cellphone, all belonging to Mr. Tinsley. Plus, there were trace evidence collected."

"What about the body of Mr. Tinsley? Ebony treaded lightly. "Was there anything peculiar about the way that he was found?"

Scarlatti was back on her feet. "Objection, Your Honor! Prosecutor is strategically manipulating the testimony of this witness."

"Your Honor," Ebony stood her ground. "This question was legally within guidelines of Direct Examination."

"Objection overruled," the judge made his decision. "Carry on, Ms. Davis!"

"Thank you, Your Honor!" Ebony offered as the attorney retook her seat. "Mr. Shivers, you may answer the question."

"Well, I wouldn't say that the find was peculiar," Shivers went on. "However, the subject was found with some kind of plastic tube around his neck."

"So, after the collecting and processing of the evidence, was anyone arrested and charged for whatever crimes were committed against Mr. Tinsley?"

"Yes. An arrest was subsequently made."

"Can you give me a name, or names of whomever was arrested in this case?"

"The detective darted his eyes at the defense table. "There was only one arrest," he said. "Mr. Vernon Webb."

"Do you see the person in this court room today?"

He nodded. "Yes ma'am."

"Can you point him out, and tell me what he's wearing?"

"He's seated at that table," Shivers said, pointing. "Wearing a dark green suit."

Ebony looked to the judge. "Let the record reflect that the witness has identified the defendant, Vernon Webb!"

"Reflected," Jackson responded.

"Mr. Shivers," Ebony resumed. "What are the charges that were brought against Mr. Webb?"

The detective cleared his throat before ranting off: "Kidnapping, false imprisonment, sexual assault, and first-degree murder."

"How did the sexual assault come about?"

"There was DNA found around the private area of the subject," answered the detective. "Once the technicians analyzed and confirmed the host of the specimen, we obtained a warrant, then commenced to arrest Mr. Webb."

Thank you, Mr. Shivers!" Ebony said collecting the file. "No further questions, Your Honor."

The judge looked over to Scarlatti. "Cross?"

"Yes, Your Honor," she answered.

The attorney got to her feet and made for the podium as ebony headed to the State's table. Figuring the attorney wanted the file, she held it out to Scarlatti, who gave it a mere glance in passing. However, Ebony didn't let it bother her. She took her seat and found herself sexually eyeing the curves of the Italian woman, who was looking ravishing in her dark green snug fitted skirt.

"Mr. Shivers," Scarlatti started. "I'm Attorney Rebecca Scarlatti, counsel for the defendant, Mr. Vernon Webb, and I only have a few questions for you. My first question is: how long have you been a homicide detective?"

"I received my detective badge in two thousand and sixteen," he answered, proudly.

"Roughly eight years ago, right?"

He nodded, "Yes."

So, this would pretty much make you highly acute to all policies and procedures, correct?"

"I mean, I'm very familiar with the requirements of my profession," Shivers gave with a shrug.

"One moment," the attorney said before moving towards the State's table.

Ebony pretty much had an inkling of what Scarlatti was up to. She just knew which file the attorney was about to ask for, though she didn't ask for anything. Instead, she, as Ebony figured, selected the medical examiner's, then spun on her heels without giving either prosecutor a mere once over. Yet and still, Ebony knew where this was going.

"May I approach the witness, Your Honor?" Scarlatti asked.

"You may," Jackson responded.

As she did, the attorney placed the file down in front of the detective, then took her place behind the lectern.

"Mr. Shivers," she began. "What I placed in front of you is what's been marked as State's Exhibit Four. I want to give you a brief moment to look that over."

Shivers looked through the contents of the folder before looking back up at the attorney.

"Mr. Shivers," Rebecca went on. "Could you tell the court what you were just looking through?"

"It's a copy of the M.E.'s report," he answered.

"The medical examiner's report?"

He nodded. "Yes, ma'am."

"Now, you did testify that you were highly familiar with all the policies and procedures right?"

"That's correct."

"I want you to study a few of those signed documents," she told him. "The signature section."

He sifted through a few of the documents, then gave her a questionable look.

"How many signatures does it take to certify a medical examiner's report?" Scarlatti dove right in.

Ebony had already expected this, but there was nothing she could do to prevent it. Knowing the attorney's reputation, she was going to use the M.E.'s report as a tool to get her client acquitted.

"There should be three signatures on each document," Shivers now answered, flipping through

the pages again.

"How many do you have there?"

"There's only two on each one," he told her. "I honestly hadn't noticed that in the beginning. I mean, I don't usually look at the signatures when I receive these reports, so I guess it's a mistake on my behalf."

"It's not a mistake on your behalf, Mr. Shivers," Scarlatti offered, sweetly. "However, being the professional investigator that you are, whose highly familiar with all policies and procedures, would a missing signature render a report inconclusive?"

The detective lingered.

"Don't forget that you are under oath, Mr. Shivers!" she reminded him.

"Yes," Shivers finally answered. "I suppose a medical examiner's report is not official without all three signatures."

"Nothing further, Your Honor."

Retrieving the file, Scarlatti approached the State's table with a mischievous grin on her face in which Ebony should have been offended by, but she wasn't. In fact, she was turned on by the gorgeous Italian dame. Upon retrieving the file, she winked at Scarlatti, whose grin instantly turned into a frown. Perhaps she wasn't into women.

***

"I still believe that you can pull it off," Aaron Taylor said, as he and Ebony were strolling through the parking garage.

"Why do I feel like you're just telling me this?" Ebony asked, looking into his eyes. "I appreciate the pep talk, Aaron, but…"

"I'm not just telling you this," he cut her off. "You're the daughter of the great Tyrone Davis, who beat the pants off the great Greg Bush, who was more formidable than Scarlatti.

"I understand all that, Aaron," Ebony said as they reached her car. "But I'm not my dad. I can never be him or anything like him. If Scarlatti wins, it won't be the end of the world. It'll just be another victory for her."

"You're right," he gave in. Then after taking a deep breath, he lingered a few seconds before asking. "Do you have anything planned for Saturday?"

"I'd let you come over, tonight," she said, knowing what he wanted. "But I have to take a little road trip."

Ready to be on her way, Ebony stood on her toes and kissed him on the mouth. "Goodnight, Aaron!"

He opened the driver's door for her. Ebony got in placing the briefcase on the seat beside her. Once Aaron closed the door and moved on, she pulled Rick's phone number up on he [hone.

"I'm listening," Rick's voice came through the earpiece.

"Why Bibb?"

"It has something to do with this case," Ebony answered.

"Anyway, I was calling to see if it was safe for me to go alone."

"You're being sarcastic right?" he asked with all seriousness.

"No, I am not," she said. "I'm en route to Bibb County right now. I also called to inquire about my star witness."

"Everything's good."

"It better be! Just make sure you handle the transportation part!"

Chapter 16

"State, you may call your next witness."

Ebony got to her feet. Your Honor, the State would like to call Chief Medical Examiner, Todd Bellamy, to the stand."

"This will be one of the add-ons, right?"

"Yes, Your Honor."

Judge Jackson looks to Deputy Taylor. Bailiff, bring in Mr. Bellamy!"

Taylor exited the courtroom, momentarily returning with a black male, who was 6'2", dark complexion and clad in a powder-blue suit. The forty-seven-year-old man took to the stand and was sworn in by Taylor. Once this procedure was complete, Judge Jackson looked to Ebony.

"State, your witness," he prompted.

Ebony rounded her table and stood behind the lectern. "Good morning, Mr. Bellamy!"

"Good morning!" he responded with a nod.

"I am Ebony Davis," she said. "The prosecutor in this case. For the record, Mr. Bellamy, could you tell the court how you're employed."

"I am the chief medical examiner at the Northside Hospital, in Bibb County.

"Did you hold this same position on the seventh of March, two thousand and twenty-three thousand?"

"Yes, I did."

"One second," Ebony said, then moved towards her table. Retrieving the medical examiner's report, she turned to face the judge. "Your Honor, may I approach the witness?"

"You may," he answered.

Ebony placed the file in front of the M.E. then stepped back behind the podium.

"Mr. Bellamy, I just placed a folder in front of you. Once you take a moment to view its contents, I want you to tell the court what that is."

"Okay," he replied, then began looking through the file. Finished, he looked up at the prosecutor. "This is the post-mortem report done on Malcom Tinsley by Dr. Winters."

"Do you remember signing that report?" she questioned.

"No," he answered. "In fact, I was out on a sick leave at the time. I think the report landed on my secretary's desk, and she forwarded it, unaware that I, or, an active supervisor, hadn't signed it.

"Was this ever rectified?"

"Yes, it was."

"Do you mind telling me when?"

"On yesterday," he answered. "I was working late, when I received a visit from the prosecutor."

"That would be me, right?"

"Yes."

"Go on!" she urged.

"After you explained to me what the situation was," he resumed, "I pulled the file up from our archives, and went over it. Seeing that Mr. Winters' analysis was good, I certified it with my John Hancock, then made a copy for the court,"

"One second, Mr. Bellamy," Ebony said, then approached the judge. "Your Honor, may I approach the witness?"

"You may," he responded.

Approaching, Ebony placed the folder on top of the one that was already in front of the medical examiner, then took locus behind the podium.

"Mr. Bellamy, I just placed another folder in front of you. Can you tell the court what that is?"

He flipped through the contents before answering. "It's the same copy of Mr. Winters' analysis that I validated on yesterday."

"What's the difference between the two?"

"Nothing," Bellamy answered. "Except one has my signature and the other doesn't."

Ebony turned to the judge. "Your Honor, the State would like to publish the additional file into evidence as State's Exhibit Four-A."

"Any objections from the defense?" Judge Jackson asked.

"Yes, Your Honor," Scarlatti replied from her seat. "I'd like to view this new file, if I may."

Before the judge could make a ruling, Ebony's feet were already in motion. Retrieving the file, she crossed over to the defense table, and handed it over to the attorney, who took her precious time looking over the documents before handing it back.

"Does the defense object to this file being admitted into evidence?" the judge inquired.

Scarlatti answered, "No, Your Honor."

"Thank you, Your Honor!" Ebony handed the folder over to Briggs, then turned back to the judge. "Your Honor, at this time, the State has no further question for Mr. Bellamy."

Jackson looked to Scarlatti. "Cross?"

"No, Your Honor," she answered.

"May this witness be released?"

"Yes, Your Honor," answered Ebony, who retrieved the other file from the witness stand before heading back to her table.

"Mr. Bellamy," the judge spoke. "You may be released. State, you may call your next witness."

"Your Honor, The State calls Ms. Stephanie Bogart, the mistress of Mr. Vernon Webb, to the stand."

Judge Jackson looks to Aaron Taylor. "Bailiff, bring in Ms. Bogart!"

While Taylor was escorting the medical examiner out of the courtroom, Ebony took a seat, and shot a furtive glance over at the defense table to see Webb conferring with his attorney, with a look of disbelief on his face. Of course, he was telling her that he didn't know anybody by the name of Stephanie Bogart. Ebony was just hoping that Rick had prepped the woman well enough to withstand the cross examination of Rebecca *'the Genie'* Scarlatti.

Moments later, Taylor returned with Stephanie Bogart, who didn't look as though she was an abuser of any kind of drug or alcoholic substances, as she was draped in a gray, pin-striped pantsuit, and pink blouse. Her sandy-brown hair was cut into a bob that barely graced her neck, and she peacocked to the witness stand with the gait of a royal heir.

"Please, raise your left hand, and place your right hand on the Bible!" Taylor said, preparing to swear her in. "Do you swear to tell the truth, the whole truth, and nothing but the truth so help you God?"

"I do," she answered, shifting her green eyes over to Webb.

"You may be seated," Taylor told her.

"Mrs. Bogart," the judge took over. "Please say your full name and spell your last name out for the court!"

Stephanie Marie Bogart," she complied. "B-O-G-A-R-T."

Jackson looks to Ebony. "State, your witness."

"Thank you, Your Honor!" Ebony said getting up from her seat and approaching the lectern. "Ms. Bogart, I am Ebony Davis, the prosecutor in this case, and I'm going to be questioning you about your relationship with Mr. Webb, but first, I need you to tell me if you see Mr. Webb in this courtroom."

"Yes, I do," she answered.

"Could you point him out, and tell me what he's wearing?"

She pointed one of her manicured fingers at the defense table. "He's sitting over there, wearing a green shirt."

Ebony regarded the judge. "Let the record reflect that the witness has identified the defendant, Vernon Webb."

"Reflected," he replied.

"Ms. Bogart," Ebony resumed. "What was the relationship between you and Mr. Webb?"

"We were dating."

"What does that mean?"

"We got together, occasionally," she answered with a slight shrug. "You know, whenever he could find the time."

"Did you know that Mr. Webb was married?"

Bogart gave another shrug. "I mean, he's mention her, but I never questioned him about his personal life."

"So, how long have you two been seeing each other?" Ebony posed.

"For about nine months," she answered. "We didn't hang out or anything like that. Most of our time was spent in hotels and sometimes the back seat of his car."

"Did you guys ever talk, or was it all based on intimacy?"

"We were quite big on talking?"

"Oh yeah?" Ebony feigned surprise. "Share any dark secrets?"

The woman took a deep breath before saying, "We've talk about things. I won't say that we shared dark secrets, but Vernon did tend to talk a little too much when he's drinking."

"What are some of the things he'd talk about under the influence?"

Stephanie Bogart drew another breath, then cast her eyes down to her hands that she fidgeted with in her lap, while slowly shaking her head in an award-winning performance that Ebony found herself proud of. She wanted to eg the women on but chose to let her rule her own stage.

"He, um…" she broke the silence with her voice cracking, making sure to throw in a sniffle that preceded a single tear. "He made a terrifying confession to me one night."

"Take your time, Ms. Bogart!" Ebony offered in a show of empathy. "What kind of confession did Mr. Webb make to you?"

"At that time," Bogart resumed in a much lower tone. "I don't think he was fully aware that he was making a confession, or to whom he was making it to, but he admitted to having done horrible things to the boy before…"

"Wait a minute!" Ebony held a hand out for emphasis. "Mr. Webb confessed to doing bad things to a boy. Did he ever say the boy's name?"

She looks up at Ebony with tears streaming down her face. "He said the boy's name was Malcom."

Ebony paused for effect and to let Stephanie dab at her crocodile tears. Then she asked: "Did Mr. Webb say what kind of bad things he'd done to Malcom?"

Bogart shook her head like a small child. "No. Only that he'd done bad things to him."

Shifting her weight, Ebony asked: "Mr. Bogart, what made you come forth with this testimony?"

"It was my conscience," she admitted. "What Vernon did was wrong, and he should pay for his actions."

"Thank you, Ms. Bogart!" Ebony looks to the judge. "No further questions."

Jackson looked to the defense table. "Cross?"

"Yes, Your Honor," Scarlatti answered getting to her feet and trading places with the prosecutor.

"Good afternoon, Ms. Bogart!"

"Good afternoon!" the witness replied with a nod.

"How did you and Mr. Webb meet?" Scarlatti dived right in.

"Um…" Stephanie Bogart looked to the ceiling as if trying to retain. "It was one of the few times that I attended church services. I approached him at one of the recreational conventions and we hit it off."

"So, you were both members of the same church?"

"I wasn't a member," she rectified. "My job only allowed me every other Sunday off, though I didn't attend services on every last one of those days."

"So, while attending these services, whenever you could, not once have you encountered Mr. Webb's wife?"

"She never attended."

Ebony smiled to herself because that frivolous piece of information was obtained from a written statement made by Webb's wife, years ago, following a domestic dispute that resulted in the police being called to their home, and Vernon being arrested. She was sure that Scarlatti was unaware of the statement, if not the incident.

"Ms. Bogart," Scarlatti seemed to switch tones. "You testified that you and Mr. Webb used to spend time in hotels and the back seat of his car, correct?"

She nodded. "Yes."

"What kind of car did Mr. Webb own?"

"Shit! Ebony thought upon seeing the way Stephanie Bogart tensed up at the question. Of course, she didn't know the answer to that question because Rick didn't tell her, on the count of him not knowing, being that Ebony didn't think to find out what kind of vehicle that Webb fancied.

Scarlatti immediately turned to the judge. "Your Honor, at this time, the defense would like to move for a motion for limine."

"What are you trying to exclude, Ms. Scarlatti?" Jackson asked in an exasperated tone.

"The entire testimony of this supposed witness," she answered gesturing with one hand.

"Why would you..."

"This woman is a fraud, Your Honor!" Scarlatti cut him off. "She's never met, nor had the pleasure of spending time with the defendant, which makes her guilty of perjury."

"Can the defendant prove these allegations?" the judge wanted to know.

"Of course, Your Honor." She snapped her fingers, as if remembering something. "Better yet, scratch the motion! The defense is requesting that this witness undergo an immediate polygraph testing before continuing with current testimonies."

"Objection, Your Honor!" Ebony finally came to the rescue. "Defense attorney's request is null and void, being that she hasn't presented anything substantial to validate her allegations."

"Your Honor, Scarlatti shot back. "This woman claimed that she and the defendant spent time in the back seat of the defendant's vehicle but can't tell the court what kind of vehicle the defendant owned."

Judge Jackson looked to Ebony, who couldn't think of anything else to say. "Alright," he said with a sigh. "The court will rule in favor of the defense. Ms. Bogart, you are hereby ordered to be here at eight o'clock tomorrow morning to undergo a polygraph testing. Your failure to do so will result in a warrant being issued for your arrest. Do you understand, Ms. Bogart?"

"Yes, sir!" the woman answered in barely a whisper.

Jackson addressed the court. "As of now, court is adjourned until tomorrow morning."

With that, he banged his gravel then headed for his chambers. While the jury members filed out of the courtroom, Scarlatti headed back to her table, giving a knowing look. Vernon Webb was out on bond, so Ebony and Corey Briggs were still getting their things together when he and his attorney made their exits. At that time. Aaron Taylor approached.

"Can I walk you to your car?" he asked Ebony.

"Sure," she answered. "But, I have to stop by my office first."

Without a word to Briggs, Ebony exited the courtroom and took the elevator up to her floor. Entering her office, she closed the door, then flopped down into her chair, perspiring, though the room's temperature was quite cool. The plan of bringing in the fake witness to testify against Vernon Webb was supposed to be foolproof, but the Genie still managed to produce a monkey wrench out of thin air and put it right where she needed it to be. It was just a good thing that Ebony had come up with a contingency plan.

Disengaging the lock on her bottom drawer, ebony pulled out her pocketbook, sat it atop the desk, then quickly rummaged through it for her vial that contained er personal dosage of crush. As have become her custom, she sprinkled some onto her fingernail and snorted it into one nostril. After feeding her other nostril, she titled her head back and commenced to enjoy the rush with her eyes closed.

Knock! Knock!

Before Ebony could open her and answer the knock, the door slowly opened up on its hinges. At that time, Larry Hendrix stuck his head in before taking it upon himself to enter, carrying her briefcase.

"I'm sorry!" he apologized as he neared the desk. "Are you busy?"

"I'm preparing to leave," she told him, tossing the vial into her pocketbook. "What do you need?"

"I just stopped by to check on you," he purported. "I know things haven't been the same since…"

"Since Samantha's death?" Ebony offered after the short pause.

"Look," Hendrix went on. "If you ever feel like you need someone to talk to, let me know."

"Thanks Hendrix!" She offered a plausible smile. "I'll take that into consideration."

He gave a nod. "Okay, see you tomorrow."

When the prosecutor left, Ebony sat back, wondering about his unceremonious visit. He wanted to say something to her, and Ebony didn't think it had anything to do with the late Samantha Gordon. She collected her things, then locked her office on her way to the elevator, where she pressed the button to ring for it. Right then, the steel doors slid open to Aaron Taylor, who was about to step off, but stopped.

"Oh!" he exclaimed. "I was on my way to see if you were ready."

"Is that your excuse?" Ebony poised, brushing past him as she entered the shaft. "Are you sure you wasn't fantasizing about having office sex with me?"

"Huh!" Aaron's face turned crimson.

Ebony only smiled as she pressed for the ground floor. Of course, it was the drug talking, though her hormones played a big part in it. In spite of all that was going on, she was determined to have sex with someone, tonight! Perhaps, Aaron was thinking the same thing because he was quiet for the duration of their trip to the car garage.

"Thank you, Aaron!" Ebony said, as she disarmed her car by remote.

"You're more than welcome!" he replied, pulling the driver's door open for her.

Closing the gap between them, Ebony stared up into Aaron's dark eyes before standing on her toes and locking her lips with his without a care as to who, or if anyone was watching. After almost a full minute of trying to shove her tongue down his throat, she broke the kiss.

"Come over to my place!" Ebony said, breathlessly.

Aaron furrowed his eyebrows. "Right now?"

"Of course."

"Can I at least go home and shower first?"

Ebony looked as though she was considering this, then said, "Alright. Just don't make me wait too long because I'll start without you."

Ebony got into her car placing her things on the seat beside her. Aaron shut the door for her, then headed for his own car. She retrieved her phone and dialed Rick's number.

"How'd she do?" Rick questioned upon answering.

"Great!" Ebony answered, reflecting on the performance that Stephanie Bogart gave on the witness stand.

"I figured she would pull it off," he said, proudly. "So, what's next?"

Ebony let out a sharp breath before saying, "We gotta proceed with Phase Two."

"What!" Rick exclaimed. "You said she did a great job Ebony."

"She did," Ebony replied, hating herself for having to make these kinds of decisions. "Also, call Bull and let him know that he has the green light on that. I want it done, tonight!"

Chapter 17

After getting off the phone with Ebony, Rick, who was seated in the dining area of a Ruby Tuesday's restaurant, immediately phoned Bull. They've been inactive since liquidating the governor and the Solid Nation members, and Rick was hoping that it stayed that way for some time. He was definitely hoping not to receive that particular call from Ebony.

"What's good?" Bull baritone voice boomed through the earpiece.

"Nothing," Rick answered. "Everything's all bad. Ebony wants me to initiate Phase Two."

"What!" Bull let out. "So, Stephanie dropped the ball?"

"She said Stephanie did a great job."

"So, why the hell…"

"I didn't ask, Bull" he cut his friend off, now knowing what Bull was thinking.

"We need to go ahead and handle that!" Bull voiced confirming Rick's thoughts.

"We're not going down that road again, Bull!" Rick hissed, keeping his voice low for the sake of other customers. "Not right now. She wanted me to let you know that you have the green light on that. She wants it done tonight."

***

Ebony didn't know how long it was going to take for Aaron to go home and freshen up, but she only allowed herself to take a fifteen-minute shower before wrapping herself in one of her robes and making for the kitchen, where she poured herself a glass of Paul Masson. Taking a large gulp of the strong alcohol, Ebony headed back to her bedroom, knowing what she needed to add to her drink to really set the mood. She opened the drawer on the nightstand and used her fingernail to scoop crush off the pile on the saucer, stirred it with her finger, then took another sip.

"Now, we're talking!" she voiced, smiling.

Ding-dong!

Being the Door-Cam automatically draws live feed whenever someone rings the doorbell, Ebony looked over at the monitor beside he bed to see Aaron Taylor standing at the front door. Hating the fact that she never purchased the voice activating door entrance, Ebony huffed, then marched towards the living room with her robe hanging open. Not bothering to cover herself, she pulled the door open and saw Aaron's eyes instantly lock onto her exposed assets. He was wearing blue jeans and a gray sweater. When she stepped aside, he entered, still gazing at her body, which made Ebony smile to herself, but turned her on at the same time. She hurriedly closed the door against the cold air that funneled through the threshold.

"Here!" she said, handing him the glass. "Drink this!"

Before he could get the glass up to his lips, Ebony dropped to her knees and began undoing his pants. Getting them and his boxers down to his calves, she wasn't surprised to see that he was fully erect, exposing his full length, which made her mouth water. Wasting no time, she took his steel rod into her mouth and pretty much tried to swallow the whole thing.

"Ooh shit!" Aaron let out before downing the remainder of the drugged beverage.

***

Almost an hour after getting off the phone with Bull, Rick arrived at the non-descript body shop that he used to frequent when he was stealing cars as an adolescent. He already called Hamburger ahead of time, explaining what he needed, which was probably large, rotund, and dark-complexioned man; was already standing in front of the establishment when Rick pulled in. Being that Hamburger wasn't familiar with the Audi, Rick rolled down the dark tinted window. Recognizing him, Hamburger indicated the blue Jeep Landscape that he was standing near. Nodding, Rick parked beside the SUV then got out.

"Did you leave the keys?" Rick told him then regarded the jeep. "What's the word on this?"

"It's hotter than Arizona!" his friend replied. "But I did disarm the GPS tracker, so you don't have to worry about being swarmed.

"That's what up!" Rick bumped fists with him. "Put it on my tab."

"You know I will."

It took a little over 30 minutes to reach his destination, and he wasn't at all surprised to see that Stephanie was already standing at the bus stop like he instructed her to do.

"It's like five degrees out there" the Caucasian woman expressed upon sliding in beside him. She was still wearing the same attire she'd worn to the courthouse earlier.

"So, how'd it go?" Rick asked, driving on.

"Everything was going well until his attorney asked me what kind of car he owns," she huffed, shooting him an accusing look. "Why didn't you tell me what kind of car he owned?"

"Because I didn't know," Rick said slow wondering why Ebony didn't furnish him with this information.

"Well," Stephanie went on. "The attorney requested that I be scheduled for a polygraph testing in the morning."

"Did the judge grant it?" Rick asked, parking on a sloping street facing a dead end that consisted of kudzu and trees growing from a ditch.

"Of course, he did!" she answered taking a quick glance around. "Vernon has a great attorney!"

"Here you go! Rick pulled a sealed letter-sized envelope from his inner pocket, handing it to her. "Just as we agreed."

"But, what about tomorrow?"

Rick shrugged. "Don't show up."

"Okay," Stephanie said slowly, peeling the envelope's flap open with one of her fingernails. Inside were a stack of bills and a compressed package of crush. She pulled the package, then looked over at him. "Do you mind if I try some of this out?"

"Help yourself," he told her, gripping his manhood through his pants. "Once you're done, I have something else you can try out."

A broad smile spread across her face as she seemed to undress him with her eyes. "So, that's why you parked here. Okay, I'll take of you in just a sec."

Humming the tune to a song that Rick never heard of Stephanie commenced to puncture a hole in the package wide enough to slide the fingernail of her pinky inside. After treating he nose, she tilted her head back with her eyes closed allowing the drug to take effect. When her body started to convulse uncontrollably, Rick knew what was taking place. Then with her eyes still tightly shut, blood began to trickle from her nose and mix with the foam formed around her mouth.

Seeing that the effect of the poison was irrevocable, Rick pulled a handkerchief from inside his coat, and began wiping the steering wheel down. He took the envelope full of bills from her grasp, stuffed it back inside his pocket then pushed his door open. After wiping the door down, he grabbed the gearshift with the cloth and pressed his foot down of the brake with his foot outside of the SUV. With one last look at

Stephanie, whose body was no longer convulsing, but breathing slowly with her chin rested on her chest, Rick threw the gear into drive, then stepped back. He watched the jeep as it coasted toward the end of the street and disappeared into the ditch with a loud crash.

***

"This is her right here!" Bull said when he saw the gray Volvo Reign approach and pull into the driveway of the house that he was parked across the street from.

At 8:17PM the moon had already taken the place of the sun, and Bull had been parked in the same spot since 6:24PM He didn't know what time the woman would make it home, but he had no problem collecting Willie and Poncho, who were both accompanying him in the dark blue GMC van, clad in dark clothing with ski masks rolled up on top of their heads.

"Y'all already know what to do," Bull now said then looked to the one positioned in the rear. "Poncho, leave that door open, so y'all can just throw her in! Go!"

Like a pair of trained SEALS they both pulled their masks down over their faces then hopped out, Poncho exiting the rear leaving the sliding door open as told.

By this time, the attorney was exiting her car, carrying a briefcase with her pocketbook hanging off one shoulder. Not once did she look around for any potential threat of danger as she moved toward the front door of her home. The woman was about seven feet from her door when Willie and Poncho closed in on her. What happened next caught Bull by surprise as he watched the scene from behind the wheel of the van.

Scarlatti did a quick spin, turning herself to face-off with the goons. Just then, Bull saw a burst of spray come from something she had in her hand, which was pretty much some kind of defense spray. He could hear Poncho and Willie cry out as they stopped in their tracks, covering their faces with their hands. Once they were temporarily blinded, the bold attorney brought her right foot up and into Poncho's groins. Just as he was collapsing from the blow, she did the same to Willie. Only taking a few seconds to watch them grovel around on her front lawn. Scarlatti turned and entered her house as if none of this had taken place.

Chapter 18

The following day, Ebony took a look at the defense table and for the umpteenth time wondered why Rebecca Scarlatti was even sitting there when she was supposed to have gone missing last night. All she could think of was Bull and how rotten he's been acting lately, and the disgusted looks he'd thrown her way when he thought she wasn't paying attention. Scarlatti's presence only implied that Bull had become rebellious, and that Ebony was going to have to put him down like a rabid dog.

"The witness hasn't shown up yet, Your Honor," Aaron Taylor announced upon re-entering the courtroom after being sent to retrieve Stephanie Bogart, who was scheduled to undergo the polygraph testing before the trial resumes.

"Thanks, bailiff!" Judge Jackson looked out at Ebony and Scarlatti. "The witness not being here is not enough to hinder this preceding any further. Does either the State or the defense disagree?"

"No, Your Honor," Rebecca Scarlatti spoke up, getting to her feet. "At this time, the defense wishes to rehash its request for a motion for limine, plus an additional motion to dismiss all charges against the defendant."

"I understand that the defense wishes to exclude any and all testimonies made by this missing witness, am I right?" Jackson asked.

Scarlatti nodded, "Yes, Your Honor."

"And what's your reason for the motion to dismiss?"

"Your Honor," Scarlatti answered. "This woman showed up out of thin air, offering to testify against the defendant. When asked about the kind of car the defendant owns, she couldn't answer the question."

"Your Honor," Ebony intervened from her seat. "A witness failing to answer one question does not substantiate a logical reason to grant a motion to dismiss."

"She's right, Scarlatti," the judge conceded. "As of now, I'm going to deny your motion to dismiss with and additional charge to the jury."

"Thank you, Your Honor!" Scarlatti said, taking her seat.

Jackson regarded the jury members. "Ladies and gentlemen of the jury, the court is charging you all to disregard testimony given by the witness, Ms. Stephanie Bogart on yesterday. Anything she said should not affect your opinions when you go back to deliberate." He looked to Ebony. "State, you may call your next witness."

"Your Honor," she replied. "At this time, the State rests."

"Very well!" He turned to Scarlatti. "Will the defense be putting up any witnesses?"

"Yes, Your Honor." She got to her feet. "The defense would like to call the defendant, Mr. Vernon Webb, to the stand."

***

After Scarlatti conducted her direct examination on her client, and Ebony passed up on cross examination, Judge Jackson granted an hour recess, in which Ebony used the time to journey off to her office.

Ebony was hungry, but her urge for a hit of crush seemed to surmount her need to nourish her body. Now, she was seated behind her desk, treating her nose. Afte taking a heavy dosage, she titled her head back with her eyes closed, taking a moment to enjoy her high. It seemed like Ebony's eyes were closed no longer than a few seconds when she was startled by her office door being abruptly pushed open. However, she wasn't surprised to see that Aaron was the unruly intruder. Plus, the look on his face was highly expected, considering the cold stares he'd been giving her all morning.

Boom!

Slamming the door behind him, Aaron approached the desk and stood looking down at her with eyes that could burn a hole through metal.

"How may I help you, Aaron?"

"You drugged me last night!" he accused, pointing a finger at her. "What was in that glass?"

"Paul Masson," she answered simply.

Aaron leaned forward placing his hands palm down on the desk. "Don't play with me, little girl! I'm in my right mind to crush your head in!"

"Crush my head in," she voiced, thoughtfully, then began punching keys on her keypad. "Let me look that up. Oh! Here it is!"

Ebony turned the monitor to face him. When Aaron saw the video collage that contained several pictures at multiple angles of him naked, and passed out on her bed his expression went from menacing to apprehensive. Straightening his posture, he took a couple of steps back.

"I was thinking of calling this video, *Naked and Afraid*," Ebony resumed with a smile. "What do you think of that Mr. Taylor?"

"What kind of game are you playing?"

Her eyebrows went up. "Game? Oh, I can assure you that this is not a game. With just one push of a button, not only would a copy of this go to your wife's divorce attorney but it would grace the screen of every computer in this building. Especially Judge Jackson's."

"But why would you do that?"

"That's a question I don't intend to answer," she said, pressing the sleep button on her keypad then leaning back in her chair. "However, I can make this all go away, but you'll have to do something for me. Deal or no deal?"

***

At the conclusion of recess, Vernon Webb's trial resumed with closing arguments. Considering how long it took to close out, Judge Jackson charged the jury, then adjourned for the day promising to let the jury members begin deliberations on Monday, being that it was Friday.

While conducting her closing argument, Ebony noticed that Aaron was reluctant to look in her direction, but Scarlatti seemed to be studying her intently with unreadable eyes. She was thinking about this, now as she entered the parking garage headed for her car. Although Ebony couldn't read Scarlatti's expression, she knew something was there. Perhaps, the attorney could feel a defeat coming on. Ebony mentally toyed with the idea, which put a smile on her face.

Deactivating the alarm and starting the engine with her key fob, Ebony was just pulling the driver's door open when she heard heavy footfalls quickly approaching from behind her. Before she could turn around to see what was going on, she felt an arm wrap around her waist, before a piece of cloth was pressed over her mouth and nose. With her keys and briefcase clattering to the ground, she tried to put up a fight, but the strong chemical element wafting off the rag seemed to have a rapid effect that immediately numbed her senses until her body finally went limp, and darkness overtook her.

***

Smack!

"Aah!" Ebony cried out after feeling the impact to the left side of her face.

Ebony knew that she'd been slapped, but couldn't tell by whom, being that her eyes were still shut tight. Forcing them open, the first thing she noticed was that she was bound to a wooden chair, whereas her legs were bound to the legs of it by her ankles, and her arms bound to the arms of it by her wrists. The next thing she noticed was a man standing directly in front of her. Slowly lifting her eyes, she studied his expensive loafers up to his expensive black suit and tie. Of the Caucasian descent, he looked to be in his mid-fifties with his jet-black hair slicked to the back.

Chancing a glance around, she saw that they were in some kind of office with four floor-to-ceiling windows that were all obscured by blinds. There was a cluttered, rust-spotted, metallic desk directly behind the man before her. Plus, there were two other men, both standing off each side of her. One of the men was accompanied by a woman whose eyes Ebony instantly locked on to, being that she was giving Ebony that same inscrutable look she'd been giving her all day. After a brief moment of staring into her soul, Rebecca Scarlatti said something in Italian to the man closed to Ebony, who stepped aside for her to take his spot.

Scarlatti was still wearing the same attire that she had on in court today. Stopping in front of Ebony, with her hands behind her back, the defense attorney leaned forward until her ace was just inches from Ebony's

"I'm going to be real brief, Davis," Scarlatti spoke in a mild tone. "Whether you make it out of here dead or alive is totally up to you. Understood?"

"What do you want Scarlatti?" Ebony held her ground, though she was beginning to feel Scarlatti intentions were to kill her to prevent losing the trial to her, which was what Ebony had planned for the attorney, but Bull refused to carry it out.

"Last night," Scarlatti resumed now standing erect. "I was attacked by a pair of wanna be goons in my front yard."

Ebony knew that the pause was meant to garner a reaction from her, but she held every muscle in her face at bay maintaining her initial expression.

"It was a desperate attempt," she went on. "Just like putting that bogus witness on the stand to testify against Webb. You are indeed your father's daughter!"

Ebony remained quiet.

"However," Scarlatti was finished. "I'm willing to turn a blind eye to your misdeeds. In fact, those are your two strikes. After today, if anything happens to me—whether I break a nail or get struck by lightning—my family is going to come after you, and those old ass men you have working under you. I hope I made myself very clear."

Without waiting for a response, Scarlatti spoke in her native tongue to the same man who said something to one of the others. Ebony kept her eyes on Scarlatti so she couldn't tell what was going on behind her.

Seconds later, that familiar smell reached her nose, which made her cringe. Shortly afterwards, the same rag was clamped back over her face. Of course, she put up and effortless struggle as the attorney impassively looked on. The last thing she heard Scarlatti say before she lost consciousness was: "I'll see you on Monday."

Chapter 19

"How'd you manage to leave your phone in the car?"

Ebony woke with a start at the sound of Rick's voice. With her head throbbing something awful, she forced her heavy eyelids open to see that she was lying atop her bed still clad in the same clothing from the previous day.

Finally pushing herself into a sitting position in the middle of the bed, she regarded Rick, who was standing at the foot of the bed holding his gun in one hand and her cell phone in the other. His expression was that of a disappointed parent, though she couldn't see his eyes for those ever-present sunglasses.

"Let me guess," Rick went on, tucking the gun into the waistline of his pants. "You found yourself going through some kind of mid-life crises, drove to a bar, got drunk, then drove yourself home. Am I right?'

"Don't you dare talk to me that way!" Ebony hisses as visions of last night's ordeal played over in her head. "Let's not forget who's in charge here Rick! You work for me—not the other way around!"

"Well, you need to start acting like it!" Rick shot back, tossing her phone onto the bed. "Sometimes, I feel like I'm babysitting."

She narrowed he eyes. "I hope you're referring to Bull! And why didn't he handle Scarlatti like I ordered?"

"He tried," Rick told her. "From my understanding, the target got the drop on the men that he was using. She roughed them up a little but didn't call the cops. I mean, I don't know how true that is."

"Oh, it's very true!" Ebony thought, remembering what Scarlatti said about encountering a pair of *'wanna be goons'*.

"And, what happened with Stephanie?" Rick went on. "I thought you said that she did a great job."

"She did an excellent job!" Ebony said with a sigh. "But Scarlatti got smart and asked her a question that neither of us could answer."

"About the car?"

She let out another sigh. "Yeah. Scarlatti requested a polygraph testing, and the judge granted it."

"But we didn't have to kill her," he reasoned. "We could've just told her not to show up."

Ebony snapped her head back as if being struck. "It seems like somebody all of a sudden has a soft spot, or am I missing something?"

"How long will it take for you to shower and get dressed?" he asked, blatantly ignoring her question.

"I don't know."

There was a concerned look on her face, "Why?"

"I'll be in the living room."

After disregarding another question, Rick exited the bedroom leaving Ebony to wonder what could possibly be on his mind. She didn't remember making any plans for today, so why should she be in a rush to shower and get dressed? Well, she didn't get a chance to shower yesterday.

Approximately 47 minutes later, Ebony emerged from her bedroom feeling rejuvenated from her long, hot shower. Being that Rick hadn't given her a hint as to where they were going, she was indecisive about what to put on. Eventually, she opted for one of her jean suits.

As promised, Rick was waiting in the living room, watching television with those sunglasses on. Ebony was sure that her pocketbook was still in her car, so all she had were her keys and cellular in her hand when she positioned herself on the other side of the coffee table, standing between him and the tube.

"I'm ready," she asserted.

Rick studied her for a few seconds, before saying: "Have a seat!"

So, we're not going anywhere?' she asked. "You made me get dressed, just to have a talk? Hell, I could've done that naked!"

Rick didn't respond, and Ebony knew that his stubborn ass wasn't going to repeat himself, so after lingering for another moment, she finally plopped down onto the recliner, and regarded him with anticipation.

"I had a talk with Bull," he said at a length. "We don't plan on doing this forever. We made a verbal agreement with you and so far, we've kept our word."

"All but one," Ebony pointed out, knowing that she wasn't going to let them go until they made good on that one.

"Well…" Rick unexpectedly removed his sunglasses and locked his brown eyes onto hers. "That's why I'm here."

Ebony's heart almost leaped from her chest. This was the moment she'd been waiting for, but something seemed a bit off about the man's demeanor. She didn't know if he was about to give up the name of her mother's murderer or admit to having done it himself.

"I already told you about the John Carpenter situation," he resumed. "About your mom contracting HIV from him and passing it on your dad."

"Did he send you or Bull?" Ebony plunged right in, already accepting the fact that her father orchestrated her mother's murder. Now, it was time for the triggerman to be revealed.

"Neither one of us."

"Stop beating around the bush Rick!" she voiced. "Who did he send? Was it Ellen Martinez?"

Rick remained silent, but at the mentioning of the attorney's name, his eyebrows did a slight dip, which indicated that she'd guess right.

"I knew that something was up with her," she went on. "It's like she was afraid that I may somehow find out about what she's done. If I'm correct, she's familiar with you and Bull, right?"

"Pretty much."

"Has either of you been in contact with her?"

"I haven't," Rick told her.

Ebony tilted her head to one side. "So, Bull has?"

"I don't know for sure," he answered. "I mean, I don't see any reason why he should."

"The briefcase full of money," Ebony said almost to herself. "It was her payout, but she never received it because my father was also murdered."

She looked Rick in his eyes. "You knew this all alone."

"All I know is that your dad had called her for a job," he purported. "When your mom ended up dead, I pretty much put two and two together. Yes, it was her money, but when I found it, I was thinking about your well-being, which is why I dropped it off to your grandparents' house instead."

After Ebony didn't respond, he asked: "So, do we pay Martinez a visit tonight?"

"No," She looked at her watch. "We'll do that tomorrow. Tonight, I need you to follow someone, and you don't need Bull's company."

Chapter 20

The following night, clad in black jeans and sweater, Ebony was sitting on the edge of her bed engrossed in a video that Rick sent to her over an hour ago. In the video, it showed Aaron Taylor and Corey Briggs leaving McCoy's Country Club traversing the parking lot with their gold club bags slung over their shoulders. It was dark out, but the lot was illuminated by its many lamps. Fron the angle, Ebony could tell that Rick was recording from the windshield of his car.

Momentarily, they stopped at the rear of Aaron's Chevy Yukon, where he accessed the rear compartment door by remote. After tossing his clubs into the back, he turned to Corey, who appeared to be doing all the talking. In spite of the distance, Ebony was able to study Aaron's facial expression, and she could tell that he was feigning interest in whatever Corey was yapping away about, while periodically looking around to see if anyone was out and about.

Just as she began to wonder how Aaron was going to carry out the deed that was required of him, she saw him look around once more before reaching into the tool pocket of the rear compartment and brandishing some sort of tactical knife, its blade momentarily twinkling with the aegis of the lamps. Then just as he was trained to do in the military, Aaron jammed the sharp part of it into Corey's stomach and in one swift motion, hoisted Corey into the SUV with Corey's golf club bag crashing to the ground. After a few more jabs with the weapon, Aaron seemed to wait until Corey expired before collecting the fallen clubs. While he did so, Ebony could see Corey's bloodied body lying still. Even if he wasn't dead at that moment, she knew that he was very much dead now. When the SUV pulled out, the video ended. Right then, a text came through from Rick letting her know that he and Bull were out front.

After replying that she was on the way out, she shut the phone off, tossed it onto the bed, then grabbed her black purse off the dresser before exiting her bedroom. Knowing that the arming and disarming of her alarm system is always recorded in the alarm company's SCRIBE, Ebony didn't bother with setting it as she stepped out onto the porch, pulling the door shut. It was only several minutes after seven, so nighttime had not yet settled in. With only a mere glance around, she made for the gray Toyota sedan that was parked in the driveway, behind her car, with the engine still running.

"Do I need to worry about leaving my fingerprints on this car?" Ebony asked upon climbing inti the rear seat.

"We're gonna burn it afterwards," answered Bull, who was the driver, as he began backing out of the driveway.

"Do we know if she's home right now?"

"No, we do not," Rick answered. "Whether she's there or not, the plan is still the same."

Ebony raised an eyebrow. "Which is?"

"Clip the alarm and go through the back door," he replied, matter-of-factly. "Everything is your call."

Truth be told, Ebony had no idea as to how she was going to handle Ellen Martinex. Therefore, she sat quietly for the duration of the ride and allowed her mind to conjure up a million and one scenarios of how she could let things play out. She was so caught up in her thoughts, Ebony was unaware if how long it tool to reach the attorney's adobe, but when she finally came out of her thoughts, she noticed it was dark out as Bull brought the car to a stop in front of a house that had two pick-up trucks and a motorcycle in its driveway and killed the engine.

"So, which one is it?" Ebony asked, her eyes darting from house to house.

"There," Rick indicated with the tilt of his head. "The one with the G-Wagon."

Across the street, and two housed up, Ebony spotted the silver-looking Mercedes truck sitting in its driveway, though she couldn't remember Martinez driving such vehicle. This didn't look right.

"Are you sure that's the house?" she finally inquired.

"It's the address you gave us," Rick answered. "And yes, we've checked everything out. She stays there, alone."

"She has a cat," Bull offered.

"Yeah, that," Rick replied with no emotion. "Anyway, she's not home because the car is missing. We can wait for her here or inside. It's your call."

Ebony didn't need but a second to consider this. "Inside," she said.

Without another word, the two men began exiting the car. Ebony pushed her door open and winced at how hard the cold wind assailed her in the midst of stepping out but kept at the heels of them as they moved towards the targeted house.

Reaching Martinez's home, Rick led them into the fenceless backyard. Bull immediately began unscrewing the security light over the back door while Rick produced a penlight and began meddling with the security electrical wire box.

"Got it!" he said after more than a minute.

Getting up from his kneeling position, Rick went to work on the security locks which took less than a minute. It seemed that every light was on inside as they passed through the kitchen that was immaculately clean. Leading the way to the living room, Bull and Rick made sure to do quick checks of the three bedrooms and sole bathroom to make sure that no one occupied them. Like the kitchen, the living room was tidy and looked as though no one had stepped foot inside of it in a while. Choosing the recliner over either of the two sofas, Ebony sat with one leg crossed over the other with her purse in her lap.

"So, what's the plan?" asked Rick, who was leaning against the entrance of the living room as Bull stood beside the window peering out.

"I need her to not be able to run back out that door when she sees us," Ebony told him.

"She's here!" Bull announced just as headlights shown through the curtains in the window. He looked to Rick. "We're doing it our way?"

"We don't have any other choice," he answered, then regarded Ebony. "Are you gonna sit there?"

"For now," she replied with defiance.

"It's on you Bull," Rick told his friend then disappeared down the hallway.

Bull brandished his handgun then stood beside the door where the hinges were. At that time, they heard the muffled sound of the vehicle's door closing. Shortly there came the sound of keys negotiating the locks before the front door came open to Ellen Martinez, who was carrying a brown paper bag from a local grocer.

The attorney took two steps beyond the threshold and stopped with eyes locked on Ebony, though she didn't look a bit surprised. In fact, it was almost like she was expecting the encounter. Then as though she expected someone to be standing behind the door, she turned to see Bull standing there with his gun at his side.

"Hell, Bull!" she greeted, minus the enthusiasm. "It's been a while."

Bull didn't respond.

"You can come out Rick!" Ellen called out using her free hand to close the door back.

When Rick appeared and leaned against the inner hall she seemed to eye him with want.

"You haven't aged a bit, I see."

Like Bull, Rick didn't care to respond.

Ellen turned to Ebony. "I knew you'd come someday."

The statement caught Ebony by surprise, but she dared to let it show. For this was not the same Ellen Martinez, who always seemed timid in her presence. The fifty-four-year-old woman standing before her now was as confident as a racehorse standing at the starting line of the Kentucky.

Placing her keys and grocery and onto the coffee table, Ellen removed her coat, revealing blue jeans and a purple blouse. After hanging it on the coat rack beside the door, she took a seat on the sofa placing her hands in her lap.

"I already know you're not here on a hunch," Ellen continued, looking Ebony in the eyes. "I also know that you're not here for an explanation, though I hope that you hear me out anyways."

Ebony didn't reply.

Ellen took a deep breath then resumed. "I'm not gonna say that I worked for your father, but I did do a few jobs for him. I don't know what transpired between him and your mother that pushed him to want her dead, but I refused the job.

"I needed the money, but I've never taken a life before. But when I told Tyrone that I will not murder his wife, he went on to threaten the life of my mother. I know that my confession means nothing to you. I just wanted you to understand how I got entangled up in the whole thing."

The woman leaned forward ad began removing her boots. After placing them neatly beside each other, she lied down on the sofa with her feet pointed towards Ebony and her hands resting on her chest in resemblance of someone being prepped for burial.

"I'm still haunted by the memory of that day." Ellen continued, staring at the ceiling. "Your father prepped me for it. I inquired but he would not tell me why he wanted your mother dead. All I know is that he wanted it done immediately and the more I hesitated, the more threatening he became.

"I love my mother, and the last thing I wanted was for her to die for something I did or didn't do. Anyway, Tyrone gave me a spare key. I found your mother lying on the living room couch in this manner, asleep which made it a lot easier for me because I didn't have to worry about freezing up and her over-powering me."

Ellen took a deep breath before resuming. "My mom died of cancer almost 5 years ago. All I have left is my cat, Elizabeth, who's at the vey awaiting eye surgery. I'm quite sure they'll find her a nice home. Ebony Davis, I apologize to you, and I accept full responsibility for what I did."

Then Ellen closed her eyes, indicating that she'd spoken her peace and was ready to meet her maker. Ebony looked from Rick to Bull, who were both giving her expecting looks then dug into the purse on her lap. Pulling out a black glove, she pulled it over her right hand before retrieving the black Glock from the bag.

With her eyes now locked on Ellen, Ebony got to her feet, walked over, and stood over the older woman. Thinking about the crime scene photos she'd pulled up on the computer. She remembered her mother lying in the same exact position with a bullet wound to the side of her head. Ebony pressed the barrel of the gun to the side of Ellen's temple.

Chapter 21

"I know that I'll have to let you guys go real soon," Ebony said when Bull pulled his car up to her home. "To be honest, I wish I'd never gotten into this lifestyle. I thought avenging my parents would make me feel better, but it didn't."

Rick turned to face her. "So, what are you saying?"

"I'm done," she answered. "After this trial, I'm taking a long vacation. As of tonight, you two are free to do what you want. Your last payment will be on Friday. Goodnight!"

With that, Ebony got out of the car. They watched and waited until she was inside the house before Bull made a U-turn.

"Som what'd you think about that?" Bull inquired when they reached the main road. "You think she'll just let us go?"

"Hell, Tyrone used to say the same thing to his ex-workers," Bull pointed out. "Right before he sent us to take them out."

"And who is she gonna get to take us out?"

"Any-damn-body!" Bull spat. "She's a prosecutor. She could have a cop murder one of us doing a routine traffic stop. Hell, she may even do it herself."

Rick shot him an incredulous look.

"Don't give me that look!" continue Bull. "We both know that she's capable of it. He paused to take a breath. "Whatever she has planned for us, I don't plan on finding out what it is. Again, I say we should go ahead and get her before she gets us."

Rick didn't respond because he was wrestling with the mixed emotions that involved Bull and Ebony. He wouldn't deny that Bull had a valid point, but Ebony Davis was nothing like Tyrone Davis, right? She promised that she'd let them go with no harm done. Surely, she wouldn't go back on her word, would she?

"So, what should we do?"

Bull's question pulled Rick from his thoughts. He looked out to see that they were now sitting in front of his house.

"Did you hear me?" Bull pressed, "What should we do about her?"

"Let me sleep on it, Bull!" Rick finally answered. "I'll call you."

"Sleep on it!" Bull cut him off. "Do you think that I can just go home and sleep knowing that the seed of Chucky could have someone slit my throat before I awake? I can't do it Rick!"

"Well, do what you feel Bull!" Rick deferred, pushing his door open. "I'm too tired to deal with this right now. I'll call you tomorrow."

Entering his home, Rick set the alarm, he entered his bedroom, where he dressed down to his boxer shorts. After checking to see that there were no messages on his phone, he journeyed off to the bathroom. Lowering the lid to the toilet, Rick placed the phone on top of it, then turned on the hot water. Relieving himself of his underwear, he stood under the showerhead, and let the water pelt his body while letting his thoughts reverted to Ebony and Bull. Rick was highly aware that Ebony had a thing for him, and truth be told, he wanted her also. However, he kept everything professional between them out of respect he had for Tyrone and for the sake of Bull; whom he knew would've had a hard time accepting their courtship. He knew there was nothing he could do or say to convince his friend that Ebony wouldn't break her word to them, which was why he told Bull to do what he felt. Thinking about the last thing he said to Bull before exiting the car. Rick drew the shower curtain back and looked down at his phone.

"Nor-Tek!" he spoke causing the screen on the device to light up. "Activate Global Positioning System!"

"Global Positioning System activated," the disembodied voice replied.

"Locate Streetwalker Three!" he ordered.

"Streetwalker Three located."

Seconds later, Rick found himself looking at a satellite image of a red beacon that emitted from the GPS tracker device he'd planted on Bull's car. According to the signal, Bull was travelling in the opposite direction of his home, and Rick didn't need a psychic to tell him where his friend was going or what he was about to do.

***

Wearing a pink robe, Ebony exited the bathroom following a hot, 20-minute shower. After stopping at the vanity mirror to adjust the towel wrapped around her damp hair, she flopped down on the edge of the bed, and pulled the drawer of the nightstand open. The ounce of crush that she'd already been having her way with was still sitting on the saucer with a rolled-up bill. Pulling the saucer out and placing it atop the stand, she helped herself to the drug, using the bill to feed her nostrils. Feeling the sudden rush, Ebony lied back on the bed, closed her eyes and allowed the drug to put her in the mood that she's been longing for all night. For some reason, she began thinking about Rick, which seemed to kick-start her hormones. She wondered if he would be willing to have sex with her, being that he was no longer her employee.

Creak!

The creaking sound of a nearby floorboard caused Ebony's eyes to shoot open. Her vision was a bit blurry, but it began clearing up as she slowly pulled herself back into a sitting position. Bull's frame took up eighty-seven percent of the doorframe, but Ebony's attention was on the combat-looking knife he had in his hand. Although she was high out of her mind, her thinking ability was still sharp as she cut her eyes over to the dresser where her gun was still tucked inside her purse.

"What are you doing here Bull?" Ebony asked in a composed tone trying to buy herself some time.

"I'm smarter than Rick," he answered. "I know better than to think you're gonna just let us go like that. And I'd be damned if I'm gonna spend the rest of my life looking over my shoulders, wondering when you're gonna send somebody to kill me!"

"You are your father's daughter," Bull pointed out. "So, your words means nothing to me."

Already seeing where this was going and realizing that there was no reasoning with the big guy, Ebony made a move. As quick as she could, she dashed toward the dresser, but Bull managed to counter her stride.

Smack!

His large fist connected with the side of her face with the impact knocking her onto the floor. With her head throbbing and a ringing sound in her ear, Ebony attempted to gather herself when Bull lifted her off the floor and slammed her onto the bed. Then before she could try anything, he straddled her, placing the business end of the knife up to her cheek.

"This is what's gonna happen," Bull spoke directly to her face, breath conveying a hint of vomit. "I'm gonna have sex with you. Then after I kill you, I'm gonna leave with that money you got stashed under the kitchen floor. You won't need it right?"

"Get off me, Bull!" Ebony demanded, but didn't put up a struggle, lest she cause the blade to penetrate her cheek.

Bull only laughed in response as he used his free hand to fondle her breast, which made her cringe. When he began moving his hand toward her stomach, Ebony decided then that if Bull was going to rape her, then he would be having his way with a corpse.

"Move!"

This time, Ebony put up a struggle, which was futile to the giant-of-a-man. With the hand that held the knife, he punched her in the face, dazing her. Just as quick as he did that, he clamped his other hand around her neck and began cutting off her circulation.

"Nice try!" he hissed. "You might as well let it happen because it's gonna happen. Even if I gotta kill you first."

With the taste of blood in her mouth, Ebony using both hands tried to pry Bull's hand formed around her neck to no avail, as her life slowly slipped away from her. She could feel her strength waning as her lungs burned from deprivation of air.

Just then, she felt Bull's hand rip from around her neck and the weight of his body from hers. As she lay there panting, trying to catch her breath, she could hear scuffling. Turning her aching head in that direction, she saw Bull and Rick on the floor trading blows. From her vantage point, Ebony couldn't see the knife until she was finally able to move into a sitting position. It was on the floor about 5 feet from where Bull was atop Rick, who was doing his best to block oncoming blows from the large man.

Feeling that she needed to help Rick, she eased off the bed unnoticed. The knife was surprisingly light weighted with a green handle made of some kind of soft plastic substance that fit comfortably in her hand. Wasting no time, Ebony brought the knife down, jamming the blade of it into the back of Bull's shoulder. At first, he seemed to not have noticed. Then with un-human like speed, he got up off Rick in a half spin. Ebony tried to back pedal, but the back of his hand connected with her cheek, knocking her to the floor. Looking up, she could see fire and brimstone blazing in his irises, as he reached back and pulled the knife free from his fresh wound, its blade covered in blood. Ebony cut her eyes to Rick, who was getting to his feet behind Bull.

"Don't do it, Bull!" Rick voiced.

As if dismissing Ebony as a neutralized threat, Bull turned to face Rick with the knife at his side. "You didn't bring your gun," he pointed out. "So, I guess you called yourself sneaking over here to have a little nightcap with your girlfriend."

"Just leave, Bull!"

"Why?" The big guy held his arms out. "Are you gonna kill her?"

Rick didn't answer.

"I thought not," he continued, shaking his head. "You've became soft Rick. You used to be smart. Maybe, it's the beginning of Alzheimer's. It happens to old people, right?"

Rick bit down on his bottom lip.

"We've been through a lot, my friend" Bull told him. "I've never wanted it to end like this, but you took it upon yourself to jump in front of this bullet,"

Rick lunged at Bull, punching him in the face just as Bull plunged the knife into his abdomen. Rick's eyes went wide. The punch didn't faze Bull. He pulled the knife out and Rick dropped to his knees, clutching his stomach. Bull titled Rick's head back then out the blade up to his throat.

"I'll see you when I get to hell," he told Rick. "Make sure you tell Tyrone I said…"

Pow!

The right side of Bull's cranium exploded sending brain matter and mucus splattering over the floor and bed as his body dropped beside Rick, who was looking up wide-eyed at Ebony.

"Rick!" she exclaimed, draping one of his arms over her shoulder to assist him to his feet. "Come on! We gotta get you out of here!"

"What about you?" Rick posed as she ushered him out of the bedroom.

"Don't worry about me!" she told him. "I gotta be here when the police gets here. Right now, I need to get you to your car before the whole neighborhood comes outside. Do you think you'll be able to drive yourself to a hospital?"

"I can't go to a hospital," he answered. "I'll go to jail. I do know somebody who's a nurse. She'll stitch me up."

"Fine," she said opening the front door and stepping onto the porch still holding him up. "As soon as you're well, I need you to upload that video of Aaron Taylor to the FBI Crime Stoppers website."

When they got to Rick's car that was parked at the curb behind Bull's, Ebony helped him to get seated behind the wheel. At this point, she couldn't help herself. She leaned in and began kissing him. It surprised her that he was returning her affection. Remembering what was at hand, she broke the kiss.

"Make it back to me in one piece!" She told him, shutting the car's door.

Making it back inside, Ebony locked the front door then made for her bedroom knowing that she would have to put on some clothes. Entering she heard her phone vibrating atop the nightstand beside the saucer with her drug on it.

"Hello?" she answered it.

"Hi!" another female's voice filtered through the earpiece. "I am an operator from Sen-Tech Securities. Could you tell me your name?"

"Ebony Davis."

"Okay." There were keys clacking in the background. "Ms. Davis your alarm system detected the sound of a gunshot and automatically notified the local police department, whereas a unit has been dispatched to your location. Is everything okay?"

"No," Ebony answered, curtly, then disconnected. Placing the phone down, she stuck her fingernail into the white substance.

***

Still clutching his draining wound while driving, Rick came to a stop at a traffic light. Taking a look at the dark blood seeping through his fingers, he felt that he should go ahead and make the call to Sandra. With his free hand, he pulled the phone off the seat beside him and did so.

"Hey, Rick!" Sandra answered.

"Are you at home?" he asked.

"I'm just getting off," she said. "But I'm on my way. Why do you sound like you're hurting?"

"Because I am." Rick let out a cough. "I got stabbed in a fist fight."

"Good Lord Rick!" she let out. "I'll have everything ready."

Tossing the phone back onto the seat, he accelerated through the intersection. Thinking about Ebony's kiss. He was no longer employed to her, so what would become of them? Would they become lovers? Well, of course. It's not like she was dating anyone at the moment. Plus, she put her heart and soul into that kiss.

Honk!

The sound of a car's horn pulled Rick from his mussing. That's when he realized that his car was straddling the painted line that divided the road and swerved back into his own to avoid impact with oncoming vehicles.

The pain in his belly had become severe, which seemed to spread to the veins in his head. His vision was slipping in and out, which made the headlights on the other side look like twinkling stars shooting past him. Suddenly everything went dark, but Rick was still conscious because he could still hear the muffled sounds of vehicles passing him.

Honk!

This horn was much louder than the first one, but by the time that Rick was able to force his eyes open it was too late. The headlights of the tractor trailer was so close, they may as well been glued to his windshield. There wasn't enough time to veer out of the way, so all Rick could do was brace for impact. The last thing he heard was a loud *Boom!* Before everything went dark again.

Chapter 22

"Are there any issues that need to be addressed before I send the jurors back to the jury room to deliberate?' Judge Jackson inquired.

"None from the defense," answered Scarlatti

"None from the State, Your Honor," Ebony replied from her own table.

'Very well," Jackson looked to the jurors. "Jury members you all may retreat to the jury room to conduct deliberations. When you're done, there will be a court officer stationed outside the door. Let him know that you're done, and he will let me know."

As one of the three deputies escorted the jurors out, Ebony, whose left arm was in a sling was watching Aaron Taylor, who hadn't looked directly at her all morning. They both knew why, of course, Ebony figured that at any moment the FBI Task Force was going to kick the doors in and arrest him on national television for the murder of Corey Briggs. This made her think of Rick, who didn't answer his phone, when she called him from the hospital last night. He definitely didn't answer his phone this morning. She hoped that he was well. Most importantly, she hoped that he'd uploaded that video to the FBI website.

"Ms. Davis?" Juge Jackson got her attention. "Don't forget about what I said to you earlier. I commend you for coming in this morning after what happened to you last night, but when this case is over, you need to take a month off at least."

"Yes, sir!"

He addressed the others in attendance. "We don't know how long it's gonna take for the jurors to deliberate. It may take minutes. It may take hours. However, I'm asking the primary parties not to leave the building just in case we're in for a very short ride. If you do feel the dire need for fresh air, I'm asking you not to wander too far from here. See you all in a bit."

Judge Jackson retreated through the doors of his chambers. Scarlatti began gathering her things, as Aaron and the remaining deputy escorted Vernon Webb through the door that led to the inmate holding cells, where he was being held for the sake of the deliberation.

"I got you," said Larry Hendrix, who was filling in for Corey Briggs, as he assisted Ebony with placing documents into her accordion folder. "I hope Briggs stays out for another week or so."

She looked at him. "Why?"

"Because I enjoy being around you," he admitted in a more hushed tone. "I asked Hutchins about letting us work together, but I think she wants me all to herself."

Ebony smiled. "Wel, you can't blame her right?"

"Yeah, I guess not," he said with a shrug. "I'm glad that you survived your ordeal last night."

"Thanks, Hendrix!" She got to her feet. "I have to make a few calls."

Taking hold of her accordion folder, Ebony made for the exit moving amongst the throng of attendees. She made it to the elevators.

"I see you're still at it," Scarlatti whispered from behind her.

Ebony didn't respond. Just then, one of the elevators arrived. Every person inside the hallway couldn't fit onto the first shaft, but Ebony managed to, whereas she was standing closest to the entrance. She didn't expect for Scarlatti to try and squeeze her small frame inside, but she did, standing with her back to Ebony. She was so close that Ebony was actually breathing down the Italian woman's neck.

Just as Ebony was mentally questioning the attorney's sexual preference, she surprised Ebony by taking a subtle step back, pressing her buttocks into her mid-section, which instantly turned Ebony on. The ground floor came a little too fast for Ebony's taste. When the mechanical door began to open, Scarlatti nudged herself against Ebony once more before sauntering away without looking back. Ebony wanted to follow her. Instead, she stepped aside for the others that were getting off, probably on their way to the cafeteria.

By the time Ebony made it to her car, she'd already made it up in her mind that she was going to ask Scarlatti out to lunch, someday. She figured that if Scarlatti wanted to harm her, she would have done so when she had her uncles abduct her. Ebony knew that the woman was only flexing muscles, which was very commonplace.

"Leave a message, and I'll get back to you." Rick's voice came through the earpiece of Ebony's cellular, followed by the beeping sound.

"Make sure you call me as soon as you get this message!" She spoke into the device, then tossed it onto the seat beside her.

Despite what Judge Jackson said about not going too far from the courthouse, Ebony had an appointment that she was determined to make by any means necessary. The Linkton County Health Department was only a few minutes over 20 minutes away from the courthouse. Finding a spot in its huge parking lot, Ebony had only her keys and cell phone on hand as she entered the building, and marched up to the front desk that was manned by a white woman. She didn't notice Ebony as she was jotting something down.

"Excuse me?" Ebony prompted getting the woman's attention.

CRIME BOSS 4 | PLAYA RAY

"You're the prosecutor from the news!" the woman said in awe. "I've never been in a predicament like that before, but it has to be scary being attacked and having to defend yourself in your own home."

"It happens," Ebony offered with a shrug. "Is Dr. Lee in?"

"He is," answered the receptionist. "Do you have an appointment?"

"Yes, I do."

"One second." She typed on her computer for a few seconds as if already knowing Ebony's name. "Okay. It shows that your appointment at 12:30."

"He set it for 12:30 because I'm currently in trial and didn't know what time I'd be able to make it," Ebony told her. "Could you please just call him?"

After seconds of hesitation, the woman picked up the receiver and pressed a digit. "Yes, Mr. Lee? A Ms. Ebony Davis is here to see you. Yes, sir. Okay, sir." Replacing the receiver, the woman pointed. "Just down that hall. His office is on the left."

Ebony smiled. "Thank you!"

Moving in the direction in which the receptionist indicated, Ebony finally found the doctor's office. His name was etched on the glass door that was standing wide open. The diminutive Asian man was seated behind his desk. Upon seeing her, he got to his feet.

"Come on in, Ms. Davis!" he offered. "I'm sorry to hear of your tragedy. "How are you?"

"I'm fine," she answered, shaking his small hand. "Thanks for seeing me!"

"No problem." He indicated a chair across from his desk. "Please have a seat!"

She did.

"I remember your request," Lee said, taking a seat and typing on his keys. "You wanted to review medical records of your late parents. Which one would you like to start with?'

"My mom," Ebony answered feeling her heart skip a beat at the thought of what would be revealed to her.

"That would be Mrs. Lisa Davis." He tapped some more. "She doesn't have an extensive file. What exactly are you looking for?"

"The post-mortem report," she told him. "Whatever disease that the blood tests revealed."

"Okay." He tapped some more then looked at her. "Would you like to read it yourself?"

"Just tell me Mr. Lee!"

"Okay." He cleared his throat. "It was discovered that she had HIV."

Ebony nodded pursing her lips. "And my dad?"

"That would be Mr. Tyrone Davis," Dr. Lee said, stroking more keys. "Same thing? Post-mortem blood test?"

"Yes."

"He was also infected with the disease," Lee said. "Were you already aware of this?"

"Sure," Ebony forced a smile, "Mr. Lee, could you look up one more person for me?"

"I don't see why not." He poised his hands over the keys. "Name?"

"John Carpenter."

"That name sounds vaguely familiar." Lee said as he searched. "We have seven on records. Is there anything specific that you could tell me about him?"

"He was born to a Ms. Martha Riggs," Ebony pulled from her memory bank.

"Okay," Lee did further searching. "Alright, I got him, but it's not showing that he's related to you."

Ebony raised her eyebrows. "Is that a problem, Mr. Lee?"

"Of course, Ms. Davis," the doctor answered as though offended. "I can't indulge any information on a client, dead or alive to anyone who's not related to them by birth or marriage."

"How's Lina?" Ebony switched her method.

Dr. Lee regarded her sideways. "My wife?"

"Of course."

"She's fine," he answered slowly. "How'd you know…"

"It's not about what I know Dr. Lee." She cut him off. "It's about what I can prove."

He remained silent.

Referring to her phone, Ebony pulled up a photo of the Chinese man making out with a Caucasian man at one of those outdoor cafes that caters to alternative lifestyles.

"I can easily send that to Lina's Facebook DM," Ebony went on. "But why should there be 'Big Trouble in Little China, all because you won't share a small piece of information with me?"

Taking a deep breath, Dr. Lee slowly raised his eyes from the phone to meet hers. "What are you trying to find out, Ms. Davis?"

"I want to know if Carpenter was HIV positive," she said holding her hand out. "I'd also like my phone back."

He handed the phone back to her then punched in a few more keys. "Yes, Mr. John Carpenter was diagnoses with the HIV virus."

"Now was that so hard?" Ebony said holding the phone out to him. "Here! You can erase your own picture."

Chapter 23

"Are you nervous?' Hendrix whispered to Ebony as the jury members filed into the courtroom taking their seats.

"Nope," Ebony answered, truthfully.

Ever since the lost she'd taken against Scarlatti, all Ebony wanted to do was gain a win over the Italian attorney and become a force to be reckon with like her father was. Now, she couldn't care less about that life, nor the results of this trial. She just wanted it all to be over.

"And where the hell was Rick?"

"Weill the foreman please stand?" Judge Jackson spoke once the jurors were seated.

When the older black woman got to her feet, he said, "I understand the jury has reached a verdict. Is that true?"

"Yes sir," the woman answered.

"Please, read your verdict out to the court!"

"Yes sir!" She began reading from the verdict sheet in her hand. "We, the jury, find the defendant, Vernon Webb, on the count of first-degree murder, guilty. We the jury…"

At that moment, something woke up inside of Ebony. The dejected state that she was in, slowly lifted as the foreman continued reading, finding Scarlatti client guilty of every charge that he was accused of, and giving her impeccable winning streak a nice, little black eye.

Once again, she had regained hope of becoming one of the most prominent prosecutors in Georgia. Bull was dead, so she would seduce Rick into continuing his services for her, even if she had to make him her husband.

"Thank you, jury members!" Judge Jackson voiced, when the foreman was done. "The State of Georgia appreciates your services. You all are relieved of duty."

"You should be grinning like a mischievous cat right now," Hendrix said to Ebony. "The whole world probably betted against you."

"Yeah, I'm quite sure," she mumbled, adjusting her sling, while watching the jurors exit the courtroom.

***

Upon leaving the courtroom, Ebony journeyed back to her office where she treated herself to some crush before placing another call to Rick's phone, to no avail. This infuriated her, but she had to remind herself that he was badly injured. Whoever doctored on him probably has him highly sedated.

Gathering her things, Ebony left her office thankful that the arriving elevator was empty as she got on and stood at the back of the shaft. The third floor came next, and Ebony knew that she would no longer be alone, and would have to make nice for the duration of the ride. When the door slid open, there was only Rebecca Scarlatti standing there holding her briefcase. The attorney put on a smile as she entered and stood extremely close to Ebony. The faint scent of her perfume filled Ebony's nostrils and seemed to scramble her senses.

"You put in a lot of work to get that win," Scarlatti said when the doors closed. "I guess you deserve it."

"Can I take you to lunch sometime?" Ebony plunged right in, taking advantage of the opportunity.

"Maybe," Scarlatti answered keeping her eyes glued to the floor indicator.

Before any other words could be exchanged, they made it to the ground floor. When the doors opened, Ebony fought the urge to grip the woman's buttocks right before she started to exit. She was so caught up in ogling the woman's backside that she didn't notice the other woman waiting outside the elevator until she entered.

"I heard you beat her," Ellen Matinez said, jerking her thumb over her shoulder. "Congratulations!"

"Thanks!"

Nothing else was said for the short ride to the garage. Ebony didn't have anything against the woman. Especially after hearing that she was coerced into killing her mother. If putting in the same predicament, Ebony would have done the same thing.

Reaching the garage, they both stepped off the elevator. Ebony's mind was so preoccupied with winning the trial, and how she was going to proceed after today, it took several seconds for her to realize that Martinez was actually walking beside her like they'd known each other since high school. Ebony still didn't say a thing to the woman, but it was only because she didn't know what to say to her. When they made it to Ellen's car, she stopped, and Ebony continued on.

"Ebony?"

Stopping in her tracks, Ebony turned to face the older woman.

"Thank you!" Ellen said, sincerely, wiping a tear from her eye.

After studying her for a moment, Ebony took a deep breath then said, "Goodnight, Ms. Martinez!"

With that, Ebony spun on her heels and headed for her car thinking about her victory again. She wanted to share the news with Rick, but figured she would try him back a little later. Too high spirited to head straight home, Ebony drove to a nearby liquor store, where she bought a bottle of Seagram's Gin and a red plastic cup. Then she made the 23-minute drive cast to the Sun Valley Cemetery.

It was still daylight when she parked in her usual spot, which was always made for a shorter walk to her parents' plots. Killin the engine, Ebony popped the top of the gin, grabbed the red cup, then stepped out in the chill, gentle breeze.

As she moved toward the gravesites, pouring some of the alcohol into the cup, she noticed there were only a handful of people scattered about but one in her immediate vicinity, which was fine by her. Stopping in front of the graves belonging to her mother and father, Ebony tilted her cup and down the liquid in one gulp. While pouring more, she eyed the graves, shaking her head with a disgusted look on her face.

"My dear father," she snarled. "I don't know if I should piss or shit on your grave. All I ever wanted was to be like you. Now, I come to realize that I've always been like you—a fucked up individual! I hope you're happy about that,"

After taking a few seconds to throw back more of the alcohol, Ebony shifted her eyes over to the other tombstone.

"Mamma Dearest!" she used the same tone of voice. "If anybody had me fooled—it was you. I mean, I never would've guessed that you were a Jezebel. Hell, God probably didn't know."

Ebony only took a sip from the cup. "All these years!" she slurred, feeling slightly dizzy. "You had me grieving you for all these years, only to find out that you brought this shit on yourself. Just couldn't keep your legs closed, huh? I guess I got that part from you."

At that moment, she heard the sound of squeaky brake pads scrubbing at a distance behind her. Giving in to her alcohol infused mind, Ebony turned around and saw that all too familiar green older model Cadillac parking behind her car. The distance wasn't an issue. Ebony's eyes were a little blurred from the alcohol, which was why she couldn't make out the figure of the driver that climbed from the vehicle with a ballcap atop their head. The person placed something on the roof of the car and appeared to be tampering with it as though adjusting some kind of dial. Blinking her eyes, her vision seemed to clear for a split second, and she knew that she was seeing some sort of rifle aimed at her, but who was this person that's been periodically stalking her?

Clack! Clack! Clack!

The gunshots sounded distant, but she clearly saw the flashes from the barrel, and felt the bullets tear through her upper body. Her bottle shattered, and her cup fell from her grasp, but the drug mixed with the alcohol caused her body to stand rigged for a little while longer; though the force was pulling her backwards until the heel of one of her shoes dug into earth. She stumbled, crashing onto her father's tombstone.

Before taking her last breath, Ebony realized that she had no fear of dying—she welcomed it. Her mind has always been at ease whenever she visited the cemetery. Now, she was finally about to get her own permanent spot.

***

The tires of the older model Cadillac grinded against the stone pebbles of the dirt road as it neared the house that was about seventy yards across from the barn. The driver didn't have to look directly at the house, to see that his brother was on the porch, rocking back and forth, on his favorite chair, and puffing on one of his favorite cigars. Driving on pass the house, he entered the large field that had become barren after his mother's death, being that he nor his siblings had no direct interest in keeping the family business going.

Thankful that there was still some daylight he made it around to the bulldozer and drove the car into the sloping ditch that went about 8ft. into the earth. Leaving the keys in the ignition and the rifle on the back seat, he exited the vehicle and trekked back up to the surface where he stood around taking in the fresh air. He thought he would feel better after doing what he'd done, but he didn't. His mother was still dead, and there was no getting back those nine years he spent in prison fighting a rape case that the late prosecutor, Tyrone Davis managed to have brought against him.

"I hope you happy now."

Christopher Reid turned to see his brother Kevin approaching. It was surprising that he didn't hear the Dodge truck pull up.

"I didn't do it for me," he lied, facing his brother. "I did it for Momma."

"Yeah, I'm quite sure she's turning cartwheels in her grave." Kevin said sarcastically. "So, what now?"

"I'm gonna bury this car," Chris said, moving towards the bulldozer that sat beside the large pile of soil. "Then we'll talk about selling this place and moving to another country."

The End

Lock Down Publications and Ca$h Presents
Assisted Publishing Packages

BASIC PACKAGE $499 Editing Cover Design Formatting	**UPGRADED PACKAGE** $800 Typing Editing Cover Design Formatting
ADVANCE PACKAGE $1,200 Typing Editing Cover Design Formatting Copyright registration Proofreading Upload book to Amazon	**LDP SUPREME PACKAGE** $1,500 Typing Editing Cover Design Formatting Copyright registration Proofreading Set up Amazon account Upload book to Amazon Advertise on LDP, Amazon and Facebook Page

***Other services available upon request.
Additional charges may apply

Lock Down Publications
P.O. Box 944
Stockbridge, GA 30281-9998
Phone: 470 303-9761

Submission Guideline

Submit the first three chapters of your completed manuscript to ldpsubmissions@gmail.com. In the subject line add **Your Book's Title**. The manuscript must be in a Word Doc file and sent as an attachment. Document should be in Times New Roman, double spaced, and in size 12 font. Also, provide your synopsis and full contact information. If sending multiple submissions, they must each be in a separate email.

Have a story but no way to send it electronically? You can still submit to LDP/Ca$h Presents. Send in the first three chapters, written or typed, of your completed manuscript to:

LDP: Submissions Dept
P.O. Box 944
Stockbridge, GA 30281-9998

DO NOT send original manuscript. Must be a duplicate.
Provide your synopsis and a cover letter containing your full contact information.

Thanks for considering LDP and Ca$h Presents.

NEW RELEASES

BLOODLINE OF A SAVAGE 1&2
THESE VICIOUS STREETS 1&2
RELENTLESS GOON
RELENTLESS GOON 2
BY PRINCE A. TAUHID

THE BUTTERFLY MAFIA 1-3
BY FUMIYA PAYNE

A THUG'S STREET PRINCESS 1&2
BY MEESHA

CITY OF SMOKE 2
BY MOLOTTI

STEPPERS 1,2&3
THE REAL BADDIES OF CHI-RAQ
BY KING RIO

THE LANE 1&2
BY KEN-KEN SPENCE

THUG OF SPADES 1&2
LOVE IN THE TRENCHES 2
CORNER BOYS
BY COREY ROBINSON

TIL DEATH 3
BY ARYANNA

THE BIRTH OF A GANGSTER 4
BY DELMONT PLAYER

PRODUCT OF THE STREETS 1&2
BY DEMOND "MONEY" ANDERSON

NO TIME FOR ERROR
BY KEESE

MONEY HUNGRY DEMONS
BY TRANAY ADAMS

Coming Soon from Lock Down Publications/Ca$h Presents

IF YOU CROSS ME ONCE 6
ANGEL V
By Anthony Fields

IMMA DIE BOUT MINE 5
By Aryanna

A THUGS STREET PRINCESS 3
By Meesha

PRODUCT OF THE STREETS 3
By Demond Money Anderson

CORNER BOYS 2
By Corey Robinson

THE MURDER QUEENS 6&7
By Michael Gallon

CITY OF SMOKE 3
By Molotti

CONFESSIONS OF A DOPE BOY
By Nicholas Lock

THA TAKEOVER
By Keith Chandler

BETRAYAL OF A G 2
By Ray Vinci

CRIME BOSS
By Playa Ray

Available Now

RESTRAINING ORDER 1 & 2
By **CA$H & Coffee**

LOVE KNOWS NO BOUNDARIES 1-3
By **Coffee**

RAISED AS A GOON I, II, III & IV
BRED BY THE SLUMS I, II, III
BLAST FOR ME I & II
ROTTEN TO THE CORE I II III
A BRONX TALE I, II, III
DUFFLE BAG CARTEL I II III IV V VI
HEARTLESS GOON I II III IV V
A SAVAGE DOPEBOY I II
DRUG LORDS I II III
CUTTHROAT MAFIA I II
KING OF THE TRENCHES
By **Ghost**

LAY IT DOWN I & II
LAST OF A DYING BREED I II
BLOOD STAINS OF A SHOTTA I & II III
By **Jamaica**

LOYAL TO THE GAME I II III
LIFE OF SIN I, II III
By **TJ & Jelissa**

IF LOVING HIM IS WRONG…I & II
LOVE ME EVEN WHEN IT HURTS I II III
By **Jelissa**

PUSH IT TO THE LIMIT
By **Bre' Hayes**

BLOODY COMMAS I & II
SKI MASK CARTEL I, II & III
KING OF NEW YORK I II, III IV V
RISE TO POWER I II III
COKE KINGS I II III IV V
BORN HEARTLESS I II III IV
KING OF THE TRAP I II
By **T.J. Edwards**

WHEN THE STREETS CLAP BACK I & II III
THE HEART OF A SAVAGE I II III IV
MONEY MAFIA I II
LOYAL TO THE SOIL I II III
By **Jibril Williams**

A DISTINGUISHED THUG STOLE MY HEART I II & III
LOVE SHOULDN'T HURT I II III IV
RENEGADE BOYS 1-4
PAID IN KARMA 1-3
SAVAGE STORMS 1-3
AN UNFORESEEN LOVE 1-3
BABY, I'M WINTERTIME COLD 1-3
A THUG'S STREET PRINCESS 1&2
By **Meesha**

A GANGSTER'S CODE 1-3
A GANGSTER'S SYN 1-3
THE SAVAGE LIFE 1-3
CHAINED TO THE STREETS 1-3
BLOOD ON THE MONEY 1-3
A GANGSTA'S PAIN 1-3
BEAUTIFUL LIES AND UGLY TRUTHS
CHURCH IN THESE STREETS
By **J-Blunt**

CUM FOR ME 1-8
An LDP Erotica Collaboration

BLOOD OF A BOSS 1-5
SHADOWS OF THE GAME
TRAP BASTARD
By **Askari**

THE STREETS BLEED MURDER 1-3
THE HEART OF A GANGSTA 1-3
By **Jerry Jackson**

WHEN A GOOD GIRL GOES BAD
By **Adrienne**

THE COST OF LOYALTY 1-3
By **Kweli**

BRIDE OF A HUSTLA 1-3
THE FETTI GIRLS 1-3
CORRUPTED BY A GANGSTA 1-4
BLINDED BY HIS LOVE
THE PRICE YOU PAY FOR LOVE 1-3
DOPE GIRL MAGIC 1-3
By **Destiny Skai**

A KINGPIN'S AMBITION
A KINGPIN'S AMBITION II
I MURDER FOR THE DOUGH
By **Ambitious**

TRUE SAVAGE 1-7
DOPE BOY MAGIC 1-3
MIDNIGHT CARTEL 1-3
CITY OF KINGZ 1&2
NIGHTMARE ON SILENT AVE
THE PLUG OF LIL MEXICO 1&2
CLASSIC CITY
By **Chris Green**

A GANGSTER'S REVENGE 1-4
THE BOSS MAN'S DAUGHTERS 1-5
A SAVAGE LOVE 1&2
BAE BELONGS TO ME 1&2
A HUSTLER'S DECEIT 1-3
WHAT BAD BITCHES DO 1-3
SOUL OF A MONSTER 1-3
KILL ZONE
A DOPE BOY'S QUEEN 1-3
TIL DEATH 1-3
IMMA DIE BOUT MINE 1-4
By **Aryanna**

A DOPEBOY'S PRAYER
By **Eddie "Wolf" Lee**

THE KING CARTEL 1-3
By **Frank Gresham**

THESE NIGGAS AIN'T LOYAL 1-3
By **Nikki Tee**

GANGSTA SHYT 1-3
By **CATO**

THE ULTIMATE BETRAYAL
By **Phoenix**

BOSS'N UP 1-3
By **Royal Nicole**

I LOVE YOU TO DEATH
By **Destiny J**

I RIDE FOR MY HITTA
I STILL RIDE FOR MY HITTA
By **Misty Holt**

CRIME BOSS 4 | PLAYA RAY

LOVE & CHASIN' PAPER
By **Qay Crockett**

TO DIE IN VAIN
SINS OF A HUSTLA
By **ASAD**

BROOKLYN HUSTLAZ
By **Boogsy Morina**

BROOKLYN ON LOCK 1 & 2
By **Sonovia**

GANGSTA CITY
By **Teddy Duke**

A DRUG KING AND HIS DIAMOND 1-3
A DOPEMAN'S RICHES
HER MAN, MINE'S TOO 1&2
CASH MONEY HO'S
THE WIFEY I USED TO BE 1&2
PRETTY GIRLS DO NASTY THINGS
By **Nicole Goosby**

LIPSTICK KILLAH 1-3
CRIME OF PASSION 1-3
FRIEND OR FOE 1-3
By **Mimi**

TRAPHOUSE KING 1-3
KINGPIN KILLAZ 1-3
STREET KINGS 1&2
PAID IN BLOOD 1&2
CARTEL KILLAZ 1-3
DOPE GODS 1&2
By **Hood Rich**

THE STREETS ARE CALLING
By **Duquie Wilson**

CRIME BOSS 4 | PLAYA RAY

STEADY MOBBN' 1-3
THE STREETS STAINED MY SOUL 1-3
By **Marcellus Allen**

WHO SHOT YA 1-3
SON OF A DOPE FIEND 1-4
HEAVEN GOT A GHETTO 1&2
SKI MASK MONEY 1&2
By **Renta**

GORILLAZ IN THE BAY 1-4
TEARS OF A GANGSTA 1/&2
3X KRAZY 1&2
STRAIGHT BEAST MODE 1&2
By **DE'KARI**

TRIGGADALE 1-3
MURDA WAS THE CASE 1-3
By **Elijah R. Freeman**

SLAUGHTER GANG 1-3
RUTHLESS HEART 1-3
By **Willie Slaughter**

GOD BLESS THE TRAPPERS 1-3
THESE SCANDALOUS STREETS 1-3
FEAR MY GANGSTA 1-5
THESE STREETS DON'T LOVE NOBODY 1-2
BURY ME A G 1-5
A GANGSTA'S EMPIRE 1-4
THE DOPEMAN'S BODYGAURD 1&2
THE REALEST KILLAZ 1-3
THE LAST OF THE OGS 1-3
By **Tranay Adams**

MARRIED TO A BOSS 1-3
By **Destiny Skai & Chris Green**

CRIME BOSS 4 | PLAYA RAY

KINGZ OF THE GAME 1-7
CRIME BOSS 1-3
By **Playa Ray**

FUK SHYT
By **Blakk Diamond**

DON'T F#CK WITH MY HEART 1&2
By **Linnea**

ADDICTED TO THE DRAMA 1-3
IN THE ARM OF HIS BOSS
By **Jamila**

LOYALTY AIN'T PROMISED 1&2
By **Keith Williams**

YAYO 1-4
A SHOOTER'S AMBITION 1&2
BRED IN THE GAME
By **S. Allen**

TRAP GOD 1-3
RICH $AVAGE 1-3
MONEY IN THE GRAVE 1-3
CARTEL MONEY
By **Martell Troublesome Bolden**

FOREVER GANGSTA 1&2
GLOCKS ON SATIN SHEETS 1&2
By **Adrian Dulan**

TOE TAGZ 1-4
LEVELS TO THIS SHYT 1&2
IT'S JUST ME AND YOU
By **Ah'Million**

CRIME BOSS 4 | PLAYA RAY

KINGPIN DREAMS 1-3
RAN OFF ON DA PLUG
By **Paper Boi Rari**

THE STREETS MADE ME 1-3
By **Larry D. Wright**

CONFESSIONS OF A GANGSTA 1-4
CONFESSIONS OF A JACKBOY 1-3
CONFESSIONS OF A HITMAN
By **Nicholas Lock**

I'M NOTHING WITHOUT HIS LOVE
SINS OF A THUG
TO THE THUG I LOVED BEFORE
A GANGSTA SAVED XMAS
IN A HUSTLER I TRUST
By **Monet Dragun**

QUIET MONEY 1-3
THUG LIFE 1-3
EXTENDED CLIP 1&2
A GANGSTA'S PARADISE
By **Trai'Quan**

CAUGHT UP IN THE LIFE 1-3
THE STREETS NEVER LET GO 1-3
By **Robert Baptiste**

NEW TO THE GAME 1-3
MONEY, MURDER & MEMORIES 1-3
By **Malik D. Rice**

CREAM 2-3
THE STREETS WILL TALK
By **Yolanda Moore**

THE STREETS WILL NEVER CLOSE 1-3
By **K'ajji**

LIFE OF A SAVAGE 1-4
A GANGSTA'S QUR'AN 1-4
MURDA SEASON 1-3
GANGLAND CARTEL 1-3
CHI'RAQ GANGSTAS 1-4
KILLERS ON ELM STREET 1-3
JACK BOYZ N DA BRONX 1-3
A DOPEBOY'S DREAM 1-3
JACK BOYS VS DOPE BOYS 1-3
COKE GIRLZ
COKE BOYS
SOSA GANG 1&2
BRONX SAVAGES
BODYMORE KINGPINS
BLOOD OF A GOON
By **Romell Tukes**

CONCRETE KILLA 1-3
VICIOUS LOYALTY 1-3
By **Kingpen**

THE ULTIMATE SACRIFICE 1-6
KHADIFI
IF YOU CROSS ME ONCE 1-3
ANGEL 1-4
IN THE BLINK OF AN EYE
By **Anthony Fields**

THE LIFE OF A HOOD STAR
By **Ca$h & Rashia Wilson**

NIGHTMARES OF A HUSTLA 1-3
BLOOD AND GAMES 1&2
By **King Dream**

GHOST MOB
By **Stilloan Robinson**

HARD AND RUTHLESS 1&2
MOB TOWN 251
THE BILLIONAIRE BENTLEYS 1-3
REAL G'S MOVE IN SILENCE
By **Von Diesel**

MOB TIES 1-7
SOUL OF A HUSTLER, HEART OF A KILLER 1-3
GORILLAZ IN THE TRENCHES
By **SayNoMore**

BODYMORE MURDERLAND 1-3
THE BIRTH OF A GANGSTER 1-4
By **Delmont Player**

FOR THE LOVE OF A BOSS 1&2
By **C. D. Blue**

KILLA KOUNTY 1-5
By **Khufu**

MOBBED UP 1-4
THE BRICK MAN 1-5
THE COCAINE PRINCESS 1-10
STEPPERS 1-3
SUPER GREMLIN 1-4
By **King Rio**

MONEY GAME 1&2
By **Smoove Dolla**

A GANGSTA'S KARMA 1-4
By **FLAME**

KING OF THE TRENCHES 1-3
By **GHOST & TRANAY ADAMS**

CRIME BOSS 4 | PLAYA RAY

QUEEN OF THE ZOO 1&2
By **Black Migo**

GRIMEY WAYS 1-3
BETRAYAL OF A G
By **Ray Vinci**

XMAS WITH AN ATL SHOOTER
By **Ca$h & Destiny Skai**

KING KILLA 1&2
By **Vincent "Vitto" Holloway**

BETRAYAL OF A THUG 1&2
By **Fre$h**

THE MURDER QUEENS 1-5
By **Michael Gallon**

FOR THE LOVE OF BLOOD 1-4
By **Jamel Mitchell**

HOOD CONSIGLIERE 1&2
NO TIME FOR ERROR
By **Keese**

PROTÉGÉ OF A LEGEND 1&2
LOVE IN THE TRENCHES 1&2
By **Corey Robinson**

THE PLUG'S RUTHLESS DAUGHTER
By **Tony Daniels**

BORN IN THE GRAVE 1-3
CRIME PAYS
By **Self Made Tay**

MOAN IN MY MOUTH
By **XTASY**

CRIME BOSS 4 | PLAYA RAY

TORN BETWEEN A GANGSTER AND A GENTLEMAN
By **J-BLUNT & Miss Kim**

LOYALTY IS EVERYTHING 1-3
CITY OF SMOKE 1&2
By **Molotti**

HERE TODAY GONE TOMORROW 1&2
By **Fly Rock**

WOMEN LIE MEN LIE 1-4
FIFTY SHADES OF SNOW 1-3
STACK BEFORE YOU SPLURGE
GIRLS FALL LIKE DOMINOES
NAÏVE TO THE STREETS
By **ROY MILLIGAN**

PILLOW PRINCESS
By **S. Hawkins**

THE BUTTERFLY MAFIA 1-3
SALUTE MY SAVAGERY 1&2
By **Fumiya Payne**

THE LANE 1&2
By Ken-Ken Spence

THE PUSSY TRAP 1-5
By **Nene Capri**

DIRTY DNA
By **Blaque**

SANCTIFIED AND HORNY
by **XTASY**

BOOKS BY LDP'S CEO, CA$H

TRUST IN NO MAN
TRUST IN NO MAN 2
TRUST IN NO MAN 3
BONDED BY BLOOD
SHORTY GOT A THUG
THUGS CRY
THUGS CRY 2
THUGS CRY 3
TRUST NO BITCH
TRUST NO BITCH 2
TRUST NO BITCH 3
TIL MY CASKET DROPS
RESTRAINING ORDER
RESTRAINING ORDER 2
IN LOVE WITH A CONVICT
LIFE OF A HOOD STAR
XMAS WITH AN ATL SHOOTER